IT WASN'T
ALWAYS
LIKE THIS

ALSO BY JOY PREBLE

The Sweet Dead Life
The A-Word

IT WASN'T ALWAYS LIKE THIS

JOY PREBLE

Published in the United States in 2016 by Soho Teen
an imprint of
Soho Press, Inc.
853 Broadway
New York, NY 10003

Library of Congress Cataloging-in-Publication Data

Preble, Joy, author.
It wasn't always like this / Joy Preble.

ISBN 978-1-61695-588-5
eISBN 978-1-61695-589-2

1. Love—Fiction. 2. Immortality—Fiction. I. Title
PZ7.P90518 It 2016 DDC [Fic]—dc23 2015035679

Interior design by Janine Agro, Soho Press, Inc.

Printed in the United States of America

10 9 8 7 6 5 4 3 2 1

For everyone who has ever loved.

i carry your heart—(I carry it in my heart)
—e. e. cummings

DISCLAIMER:

This novel is a work of fiction. The author fully owns any historical or place errors that might have occurred in the telling of Emma and Charlie's story. If the Fountain of Youth really exists in Florida or Texas or some obscure corner of the New York subway system, the author is keeping that to herself.

Chapter One

It was gone. Dried up. The stream. The plants. All of it.

"Maybe we're in the wrong place," Charlie said, but Emma knew he didn't mean it.

"We're not." She pushed her way through the tall grass, not caring what she disturbed. Something sharp poked through her skirt and bit into the tender flesh at the back of her knee. She kept moving. The empty jars in her pockets slapped her thighs.

Maybe Charlie was right. Maybe they were just turned around or confused. This was the first time they'd come here alone. Emma herself had been only once, under the watchful eye of her father. Maybe they were lost.

But the place was too familiar. She recognized the strange little clearing at the center of the island, only there was no stream. No purple-flowered plants. If the spell or whatever it was—Emma had never settled on the right words for what had happened to them—if "it" faded, she feared there would be no getting it back, not without the plants and the water.

At least, that's how she *thought* it worked. But she

wasn't certain, was she? That frightened her, too; Emma liked being certain.

"It doesn't matter," Charlie said. He grabbed her shoulder from behind and spun her around, pulling her close, arms encircling her waist. "You were still right. We need to run. Emma . . . we can manage without the plants. I love you."

Even in the swampy heat, he looked the way he always did; that was the root of all their troubles. Tall and angular, with broad shoulders and taut arms, jaw neatly defined. Brows thick and cheekbones etched high. A wild thatch of hair that never stayed put. Brown eyes blazing with a stubborn streak, yet with a hint of that sweet silliness he saved for Emma alone, and a sparkle she'd convinced herself nobody else could see.

He'd wanted to run even before now. In this moment, she could see him glancing skyward unconsciously, consumed with the desire to fly from this place. That desire had brought them here. She'd done this for him.

On her right side, not ten feet away, the grass waved and shifted. She felt more than saw a small alligator slither by. Caught a glimpse of a coal-black eye between the tall green blades.

Emma tried not to panic. The gators were the least of her worries.

TWO DAYS EARLIER, Emma had rushed to the aviary and wrapped her hands tight around Charlie's. "Simon," she gasped. "He . . . he . . ." How even to start?

Something both horrifying and miraculous had happened to her baby brother. They could no longer hide what they'd become. They had to leave St. Augustine. Now.

"What is it, Em?" Charlie held her close, his eyes searching hers. On their perches, the hawks quieted, as if overwhelmed with the same concern. "Is something wrong with Simon?"

"I was supposed to be—to be watching him," she stammered. "But you know how he gets." She didn't have to elaborate. Simon was a two-year-old toddler, had been for over three years now. He would be a two-year-old toddler forever. Perpetually curious and naughty and needy, all of which Charlie knew full well. "He got into the benzene while I wasn't looking. I guess it was the sweet smell, like soda pop. Daddy must have left it out on the kitchen counter after stripping the paint on the wall that—"

"Slow down, Em," Charlie soothed. "Just tell me what happened."

"*Nothing.*" Her voice trembled. "That's the trouble. My brother drank *half the bottle*. Should have burned his insides. He should have blisters or be vomiting. Something. That stuff is poison, Charlie. But *nothing happened*. I watched him. Maybe he looked a little green for about a minute . . . that was all."

Tears stung her eyes, but she trained her gaze on Charlie to calm herself. His stillness was a gift, never more so than at this moment.

"He's fine," Charlie said soothingly. "That's all that matters." But they both knew things *weren't fine*. Simon's throat hadn't burned, but the world felt like it was burning, consuming her with it.

So she'd done what a girl had to do under such circumstances. When life itself stopped making sense, she'd come up with a plan.

FIRST THEY'D STEAL a skiff from the harbor. Row to the island.

That part of the plan had worked.

But the second part, the part that mattered, had gone up in smoke. They'd brought jars to dip in the stream, but the clear water had vanished without a trace. They'd brew more tea from the plants, but the plants had vanished as well, leaving only nettles and swamp grass in their absence.

As for the last part of the plan—running—that they could still do.

EMMA HAD THOUGHT the escape would be joyous. Liberating. Their parents, both hers and Charlie's, were drowning in paranoia, unable to think or act sensibly anymore. But who knew what or how grown-ups thought, anyway? They were all crazy, the good ones, the bad ones, the dangerous ones. She and Charlie would finally be free of the worry, free of all the hateful whispers. They would be *together*. That was all that mattered.

Except the stream and its plants and the world itself had chosen not to cooperate. She felt as if the island were playing a cruel practical joke, or worse, punishing her for the sin of wanting to run off with the boy she loved. Three years they had been together. But it wasn't three years at all; it was nothing. Time was meaningless once you discovered you'd drunk from a Fountain of Youth. How stupid Emma had been, thinking that if they could just get away from their families, they could stop treading water and hide for an eternity.

Now Charlie pulled her to him again, kissing her over and over until she was dizzy from it. "It's okay," he insisted. "We'll figure something out—" All at once he stiffened. His hands fell from her body. He sniffed the air. "Smoke. It's . . ."

"The Church of Light," she finished with him.

Under different circumstances, this would have struck her as impossibly romantic: their habit of sharing the same thoughts, of ending each other's sentences. And now the sudden, wary anger in Charlie's eyes echoed the thought that squirmed in her brain: if something was burning, Glen Walters and his followers had lit the fire.

They were running again even before Charlie's fingers threaded through hers.

Chapter Two

Emma pried open one eye. Her head was splitting, her tongue stuck to the roof of her mouth. She felt like she had licked the bottom of a dirty shoe—after the shoe had been dragged through a puddle of bourbon. She eased up on an elbow. The room tilted, her stomach giving a sickly lurch.

She wasn't alone in bed. There was a guy next to her. Snoring.

Vaguely she remembered having bought street tacos outside the bar from a girl with an Igloo cooler. At the time, it seemed like a solid idea. Emma had many solid ideas when she was drunk. The tacos, involving a meat substance of unknown origin, did not seem so solid at the moment.

Her reason for being at that particular downtown Dallas bar wasn't scoring high points, either. Another dead end, it turned out. But Emma kept at things, because you just never knew. Cold trails turned warmer. Hopes bloomed, well, hopefully. Things happened. People came and went.

Girls disappeared on their way home and later turned up dead.

There had been a rash of kidnappings and murders, or at least *Emma* saw it as a rash, given her, well, uniquely expansive view of time. It was a decades-long rash, a near-century-long rash. Crimes spread apart by a dozen years and thousands of miles, not close enough together in any reasonable sense for the cops to see a pattern—and who could blame them?

But recently, there had been a subtle uptick. That first girl, Allie Golden, in Rio Rancho, north of Albuquerque, four years ago. Then six months back, one outside of Fort Worth. Karissa Isaacs, twenty years old. Both living near Emma, their deaths following her as she moved east. Both kidnapped and poisoned and dumped.

And now the third in four years, right here in Dallas. Elodie Callahan, just sixteen.

There might have been more. Emma guessed there *were* more. She would like to think she was certain about that; she still prized certainty. But she'd learned many lifetimes ago that certainty was a luxury. You could shrug off the pattern, chalk the atrocities up to coincidence. A long time ago, Emma had tried that very thing.

Or you could leap into the fray and see where it led you. Move to Dallas. Poke and prod. Hone your investigative skills. See if the pattern was indeed what you feared.

Now, in the much-too-bright light of yet another day, on the cusp of yet another new year, Emma pressed her knuckles to her aching eyes. The tacos were about to make a messy reversal unless she got herself under control. Her commitment to staying off the grid? Blown to hell and back. Emma O'Neill had let herself surface once again and now she was paying the price.

So were the dead girls.

And the guy, snoring—Mason, maybe? Mike?—legs tangled in her comforter, mouth hanging open—well, he had to go.

"Shit." She elbowed him, hard, in the ribs. "Wake up. Get out."

She smoothed her hands over her rumpled red minidress. Right now it felt like one of those old burlap sacks her father had used to store feed in St. Augustine. Between the tacos and the bourbon, it didn't smell much better.

At least the dress was still on her.

Mason/Mike was shirtless, but he was still wearing his pants.

If they'd done anything, they could have only done so much. She hoped.

"Mmphff," he mumbled. Then belched.

Jesus.

"Out," Emma said, rising, pulling herself together. "You. Rise and shine. Go away." She wasn't always this inhospitable. But Mason/Mike was an error in judgment, not company. Emma didn't mind company. She did attempt to avoid errors in judgment, but over time, over history, they were inevitable. The trick was to act fast and stay pleasant about it.

He opened his eyes—blue, bloodshot—and grinned at her. "How the hell do you still look so good?" he drawled.

Matt. His name was Matt.

"Habit," she told him, pushing harder now until he rolled off the bed and hit the floor with a thump. She didn't need a glimpse in the mirror to know they were both right. Emma O'Neill might be a tad rumpled and head-throbby right this second, but that would fade soon enough. A hangover would never make a dent in the overall picture. Toxins of any kind didn't have any real effect beyond an initial jolt or a groggy wake-up. Even toxins less pleasant than questionable street tacos. Hadn't in longer than she preferred to remember.

Matt sat up, rubbing his backside. "Now why'd you go and do that?" He scratched the side of his face. His gaze was bleary. He was cute—thick blond hair and a stubbly chin—but pasty under his tan.

He'd looked better last night. They all had.

Emma thought of her friends, Coral and Hugo. Well, mostly Coral. Coral Ballard. The girl who looked like the other girls. The girl who looked like Emma.

THEIR MEETING HAD been a random thing.

The Ballard family—Coral and her little brother and her parents and a mop-like mutt named Bernie—lived in a one-story house down the block from Emma's apartment. Emma might not even have spoken to Coral had it not been for Bernie. Stupid cute dog.

Emma had always wanted one, but a dog was a responsibility she couldn't assume. A dog might call attention where she needed anonymity. Even if it was lovable. Even if it was loyal, which dogs mostly were, unlike lovable humans, who had a bad habit of betraying girls they were *supposed* to love.

Maybe she was over-identifying on that last one.

Either way, a dog was just one more thing that would die before she did.

The pup padded closer and sat on her foot.

"You live around here?" the girl asked.

Emma's gaze shifted. Coral, she noted now, was medium height, like she was. Pale like Emma, too. A slew of brightly colored vintage pottery bracelets adorned her milky arms. Her wavy hair was streaked with lots of red and a bit of blue.

Underneath it looked to be blonde . . . maybe. But even, then Emma suspected it could have been brown. Like hers, too.

"Yeah," Emma said. The pup was still sprawled across her foot. She hoped he wasn't about to pee. "Over there." She waved toward the bits of downtown Dallas skyline visible beyond the trees on her left.

The girl yanked on the leash until the puppy moved. "Sorry about that. He likes you. You should be flattered. Bernie's particular. He doesn't like a lot of people."

"Good to know." Emma turned and nearly bumped into a boy.

"Hugo!" Coral scolded, but she was smiling. She turned to Emma. "He never watches where he's going."

Hugo had a big grin. Gangly, black-haired, Latino. And friendly. Before Emma knew it, they were introducing themselves. Hugo Alvarez and Coral Ballard were both seniors at North Dallas High School. And Emma could see: Both were funny and quirky and very much in love. It was that last part that slipped through her defenses. The way Hugo casually rested a hand on the small of Coral's back. The way their closeness reminded her of a closeness she'd once had.

Coral tapped a painted nail on her chin. "Look at her, Hugo. We could be. . .

"Sisters," Hugo and she finished at the same time. They giggled.

Bernie nudged Emma's hand, then signed happily as she stroked his head.

"Seriously, though," Coral went on, "if I let my hair go back to its own color, which I totally won't—but if I did . . . Don't we look alike, Hugo?"

He nodded.

Emma shrugged. "Maybe." She rolled her eyes to make

it not true. But it *was* true. And acknowledging that—even silently—awakened in her a fierce and sudden protectiveness she hadn't been able to quell since. So she told Coral and Hugo that she was a freshman at Brookhaven Community College studying for a nursing degree. It was the lie she'd chosen for herself upon moving to Dallas.

But occasionally, she'd wished that this were true: that she was studying to become someone who could maybe save a life.

UNFORTUNATE THAT CORAL and Hugo had chosen last night—of all nights—to sneak into that same neighborhood bar.

But that's what happened when you made friends. You ran into them.

Emma kept one eye on the guy she'd followed, and the other on Matt, whom she matched bourbon for bourbon. She didn't indulge that often, but it was the holidays, and he was cute enough. Besides, the guy she'd followed, one of Elodie Callahan's classmates, seemed to be guilty only of a bad fake ID. Like she'd figured: a dead-end. And the bourbon was reminding Emma that at the end of the day—in point of fact, a century of days—she was still alone in all this.

A potent combination.

She should have left the moment Coral and Hugo sauntered in. Or told them to leave. They were underage, after all. She didn't. Among a long list of reasons why: they thought *she* was underage, too. (In a way, she was.) And cute-enough Matt? He thought otherwise. Better to let sleeping dogs lie. Or sit on your foot, like Bernie.

"You like him," Coral whispered to Emma after bourbon number four. Or five. "Don't you?" Coral was a romantic like that.

"He's all right," Emma whispered back.

"You're cute, too," Matt said, leaning across Emma to wink at Coral. He'd heard them, obviously. Then he pressed his mouth close to Emma's ear. It had been a long time since she'd felt a boy's lips brush her skin. "But not as cute as you."

She should have known better. She *did* know better. Just sometimes . . .

At least Coral and Hugo hadn't stayed long. A party somewhere, Coral said, eyes bright—and then they were gone. Emma told her to have a nice holiday if she didn't see her; Emma was going to be spending it with some of her fellow nursing students, studying for their practicums. (Translation: investigating why a girl named Elodie Callahan had been murdered.)

It was just Emma and Matt after that, his arm draped casually over her shoulders, and some mixture of anthem rock and Christmas songs . . . and four or five bourbons too many. Matt was not Charlie. Could *never* be Charlie. But Matt was there. Sometimes *there* was enough.

And now here they were.

"I DON'T HAVE coffee," Emma said to move things along. She did in fact have coffee, two neatly stored packages in the side door of the fridge: Dunkin Donuts dark roast and a vanilla-flavored one from Whole Foods. She liked them mixed half and half. In Portland, she'd favored espresso. Dallas seemed to require something sweeter. And as soon as Matt was out the door, she would brew a pot. She would sip a mug on her little balcony while she scribbled notes, and she would decide if there was anything about the Elodie Callahan case worth pursuing. Anything she might have missed.

"You look awfully young," Matt said. He stood slowly, frowning, a thin wrinkle furrowing his brow.

Matt was *not* young. Not old, either, but somewhere in the middle. Surely no more than thirty.

"I'm twenty-one," Emma said. It was the age on her current ID, basically the youngest possible age to be licensed and accepted without suspicion as a private investigator in the state of Texas, though eighteen was the official minimum. Besides, the age on her driver's license was even true, from a certain perspective. She had *definitely* lived twenty-one years. And as far as the other minimum requirements to be licensed as both a driver and private investigator—she'd met them, too, though not in any way that could be explained to the authorities.

She remembered bringing Matt home now. Remembered eating those greasy tacos. "Give me a bite," he'd said, grinning. But she hadn't shared the taco. Even drunk, Emma was particular about her food.

He'd tried to kiss her a few times on the walk from the bar, and she'd giggled, batting him away. They'd stumbled into the apartment, and her mood changed. The air was fresh inside from the little Christmas tree she'd put up this year—her small acknowledgement that it was the holiday season, fa-la-la. She'd flipped on the tiny Italian lights and forgotten to turn them off. They were still twinkling in the branches. She'd been very drunk. It had been very late.

She should have focused on the case. She should have trailed that guy she'd followed, Elodie's classmate, back to his house. Or made sure Coral got home from that party. But it was just after Christmas, almost New Year's. And even after all this time, all that loss took a cheap shot at her, and there she was: bringing someone home, someone who hadn't looked at her carefully. Who tried to kiss her while she shoved tacos in her mouth and let her pretend the pain wasn't there, who had no clue that the world hurtled forward while she stayed *exactly the same.*

Someone who wasn't—would never be—Charlie.

Matt's lips twitched. "We could go to breakfast . . ." The offer did not sound particularly heartfelt. He scratched the back of his head. The word BELIEVE was tattooed in blue on his forearm. Last night it had seemed the most interesting thing about him. Emma had almost called him on it: *"Believe in what?"* But even drunk, she'd known that this question could have led anywhere.

Now she moved toward the window. Clicked off the tiny Italian lights. She felt sticky and tired, but the hangover was already fading, as it always did.

"This was fun," she lied. He needed to get the hint. She needed to call Coral. She needed to brush her teeth.

Matt took a step toward the bedroom door. Emma watched as he patted his pockets, touching wallet and phone. She could see their indentations against his thighs. There was a spot of something that looked like *queso* on the left knee of his jeans. She tried not to think of tacos, but her stomach was already recovering, too.

He paused, his gaze landing on the ornate gold-chained pocket watch hanging from the wall by her bed.

"Didn't peg you for the old-fashioned type."

She shrugged. Maybe he meant that no one wore pocket watches these days, which was mostly true. As far as she could tell, the people in charge of the latest fashion mined the past the way *everybody* mined the past—perpetually and always.

She wanted to snatch it away, wanted him to leave now, but instead she said more defensively than she meant, "It was a gift."

His gaze shifted back to her, looking her up and down. "You know you could pass for younger. Sixteen, even."

Good, he was done talking about the watch. Now he was stuck on the age thing. Maybe he was worried he'd broken the law.

"You killed it at history trivia," he said. He paused, as if trying and then failing to remember any other salient details about the night. In Emma's estimation, this was for the best for the both of them. Matt hadn't broken the law, but he hadn't been good at history trivia, either. Or books. Or movies, except war movies.

Matt could quote every war movie he'd ever seen. Matt had a definite thing for war movies. "Wanna know what Patton said about winning a battle?" he'd asked and she'd shrugged, which he'd taken as a yes. But the bourbon had muddled whatever his answer was.

"See you later," she said now, a lie. She handed him his striped dress shirt. It smelled of beer and sweat and some kind of cologne that should have been a deal breaker. *Christ.*

Matt tucked the shirt over his arm rather than putting it on.

Then he smiled as if he wanted to say something gentlemanly, but thought better of it. Good for him.

WHEN MATT WAS finally gone, Emma stood under a hot shower for a long time, washing the previous evening away. Having grown up before indoor plumbing was a given, Emma had a keen adoration for endless hot water.

Then she dried and dressed and brushed her teeth. She flossed. Emma was quite devoted to flossing, thanks to Detective Pete Mondragon in Albuquerque, who had told her you could tell a lot by a person's teeth.

Pete Mondragon, like Coral and Hugo, had become a friend at a bad time through the unique circumstance of her existence.

They can only hide so much under expensive clothes, he'd said.

She agreed with him about that. Certainly she'd known enough people who hid their evil under fancy outfits. It didn't take her long to admit that Pete was right about the teeth, too.

In the kitchen, wearing a peacock-blue silk robe, her dark, wavy hair in a thick, tidy braid, Emma measured out the coffee. When it was ready, she took her cup to the balcony. The weather had turned, the air warm and muggy, the sky heavy with clouds. It reminded her of Florida.

Outside, Emma sipped, the flavor both bitter and sweet. Underneath the almost tropical air, she could sense there was something unsettled. Texas weather shifted like that, fast and brutal. Or maybe *she* was unsettled. The possibility of that sudden change made her think about the first time she'd turned seventeen. What would Matt say if she told him exactly how long ago *that* was? In spite of the sentiment of his tattoo—BELIEVE—she doubted he'd believe *that*. In Emma's substantive experience, people believed lies far more easily than the truth.

Chapter Three

1916

The smoke smell grew stronger the closer Emma and Charlie drew to the mainland, their tiny rowboat lurching with every stroke. Then they could see it: plumes rising, black and ominous, over the treetops. Emma averted her eyes. She watched Charlie's hands on the oars, his face pale and jaw tight, and she tried to fight back the fear. It didn't have to be what she thought. It didn't have to be the worst.

And then they hit the dock and Charlie was up and pulling her with him, the boat rocking wildly beneath them. At that point, she gave up the fight. She knew she was right to be afraid, that she should always expect the very worst.

EMMA HAD LOVED Charlie since that day when they were ten years old, the day he caught the hawk she'd allowed to escape. It was 1906 then, and Emma's head was filled with possibility in this strange new place—Florida, so different from Brooklyn, where they'd lived before. Florida was heat and light and lush plants growing. Birds and bugs and air thick as wads of cotton. Florida was where her father promised the world would be theirs.

Not that Emma had believed him, even then.

Emma's father, Art O'Neill, had moved his family to start a business—the same reason families had always moved around the country, no matter if it was 1906 or 2006 or any year in between. Art O'Neill planned to entertain the wealthy tourists who had come down from the East for the winter with the O'Neill Alligator Farm and Museum. Not a rough-and-tumble carnival-type place like those ones in the Everglades, but a real museum with an aviary where people could learn about the creatures and see them up close. If, like Emma, you weren't fond of reptiles, there would always be the birds to look at.

Her father had also hired an acquaintance—the ever-talkative Frank Ryan—to run the bird piece of things, and so Frank had moved down from Brooklyn, too, and brought his own family with him: a wife and three children, one of them a boy Emma's age. Charlie, his name was, not that she thought much about him one way or the other. Apparently he was good with birds and would be helpful in the aviary. That was all she cared to know about him for the first few months.

They would get rich, both men whispered, the way foolish men have been whispering to their families all around the country—always, since before there was even a United States. The difference in their case (and foolish men believed there was always a difference): trust. Emma's father always said he knew Frank Ryan enough to trust him.

They both saw the same need, waiting to be filled. A family need. The way Emma and Charlie's fathers saw it, families needed to be entertained with reptiles and birds. They were more than just businessmen looking for the next best thing. They were *family* men.

"A solid basis for a partnership," said Emma's father.

Emma wasn't so sure. Mr. Ryan struck her as a braggart. Everything he said began with "I," every story large and dramatic. On the other hand, he'd worked at the Central Park Zoo and the Bronx Zoo and even the menagerie in Prospect Park near the O'Neill's house, and he knew more about birds and gators than her own father did, which was mostly limited to books. Emma's father *read* everything—so did Emma— but he hadn't been much of a doer until now.

Still, she had to hand it to him; this move to Florida was a *real* adventure. Not just something he read about or talked about. Emma hoped her father was right, that the move would make them rich. Who could complain then? Money made her parents argue, that much she knew. They fought about it late at night when they thought their children weren't listening, but sometimes Emma heard, and it made her stomach clench. Having more of it would help, wouldn't it?

But how long would that take?

Her father didn't have an answer. Once they arrived in St. Augustine, he went back to reading. And now that they were stuck here, stuck in this sticky and swampy place, she wished her father would look up from his books more often.

Then maybe he'd see how her mother laughed a little too loudly and smiled a little too brightly when Mr. Ryan told one of his jokes or stories.

The man was always talking.

Didn't he know people could also be quiet? *He* could stand to read a little more. In this way, she supposed, she was like her father. She liked to learn, liked knowing how the world worked, *really* worked. People like Frank Ryan didn't care. They were happy to make it all up as they went along. Then again, people and things weren't always predictable in ways you could learn from books.

Money would help, Emma reminded herself, and if they got rich, life would improve.

So she held out hope. Her mother would admire how her father had been right. The business would do well. Florida would be the best thing that had ever happened to any of them. Her mother would stop looking at Mr. Ryan, and Emma could stop worrying. The Ryans didn't seem to have much money either, at least not that Emma could tell.

So maybe once they all got rich, everything would work itself out.

"It's going to be wonderful," Emma's mother kept saying.

When? Emma kept wanting to ask.

It was hot and humid, and there was no big city just across the bridge like in New York. Oh, Emma loved the ocean, but she could see the Atlantic back in New York. Sometimes they traveled up to Jacksonville, but that wasn't much better. Everything smelled salty here—parts of Brooklyn smelled like the ocean sometimes but never this bad—and the streets were too skinny, and it was all too . . . small. It was not an adventure, after all. The grown-ups were too busy getting the Alligator Farm and Museum up and running, too busy rounding up huge scaly gators with enormous jaws and frightening teeth.

"But the sunrises!" her mother would exclaim when Emma grumbled.

Secretly Emma found the sunrises beautiful, the way the sun rose as if from underwater, lighting everything golden. But she would reply with a sour face.

"It's just the sun. And everything tastes like salt."

Mostly Emma thought, *You spend too much time goggling at Mr. Ryan, Mama.* Thinking about it made her chest feel tight.

And so it went. Until the day of the hawk. Until Charlie.

—

"I'M GOING OUT for a while once we finish," Emma's mother said that morning. She was unwrapping a plate from brown paper, the last of their items that had been left in storage crates from the move. "Do you know that Frank Ryan says there are thousands of ibises? He says they're exquisite. He knows everything about birds, you know."

Her mother loved pretty things. Anything new and different always caught her eye. She was a pretty thing herself, her figure shapely and slim in her new shirtwaist, even after three children.

"I hate birds," said Emma, even though she didn't. But her mother was removing the wrapper from another dish, the stiff brown paper crackling as she folded it, and so she didn't hear. "Where are you going, anyway?"

"I need to get some air. I'll be back soon." Her mother fanned at her flushed face.

In addition to unpacking, they'd been cooking and baking all morning, making baked ham and yeast rolls and mashed potatoes and green beans and a chocolate cake that was now wilting in the overheated kitchen as it cooled, the icing dripping onto the cake's platter. The museum sponsors were coming for supper, and Mrs. O'Neill had outdone herself.

"You watch Jamie and Lucy," she told her oldest daughter. "Just for a few minutes. I promise."

Emma nodded, because she knew her mother would go whether she agreed or not. Another thin dribble of icing slid from the chocolate cake. The air felt heavy and full. Her hair was curling wildly because her mother had been too distracted and busy to help her plait it, and besides, what did Emma care about her hair? Or anything except finding a way to get her family to move back to Brooklyn where everything didn't always taste like the sea. It made her feel like she was drowning.

A plan arose in her brain then. Emma was fond of plans, of figuring things out and getting the right answer. She hated making mistakes, and everything about Florida felt like a mistake.

She skimmed across the kitchen and down the hall into the small parlor where her brother Jamie was playing a game of marbles with her sister Lucy. In her haste, she almost tripped over a cat's-eye marble that had rolled toward the hall.

"Jamie," she said, "take care of Lucy. I'll be right back. It's important, Jamie. Are you listening?"

He was, sort of, but she knew she had to hurry. She was already out the door before she realized she hadn't told them not to touch the ham or rolls or cake. But Jamie was eight already, and Lucy had just turned six. More than old enough to be responsible for a few minutes. That was what Emma's ten-year-old logic informed her.

Her mother might have gone to the aviary.

Emma caught no glimpse of her down the dirt road that led from their house to the museum buildings. The plan evolved. She would go to the aviary and find her mother—and if she saw them together, her mother and Mr. Ryan, she would . . . well, she wasn't sure what she would do. But it would be *something*. And then her father would know and take them all home and leave this crazy business and this foreign place to the Ryans.

Only that wasn't what happened at all.

What happened was Emma yanked open the door to the aviary without thinking about what was on the other side. There was a furious rush of wings and the bird was past her, shooting into the air before she could even take a startled breath and realize her mistake.

"Oh!" she cried. "Oh no!" She turned, latching the door behind her, but it was too late. The hawk soared into the bright blue sky, its jess trailing, wings wide and dark. Sweat trickled down the hollow of Emma's neck. Her heart beat hard and sharp in her chest. Her ankles were itching like mad because she hadn't even stopped to put on her shoes, and something in the grass had irritated them.

The hawk screeched—loud enough to make her wince, like it was taunting her.

She gaped at it, panicked, unable to move or think.

And then, as if out of nowhere, Charlie Ryan strode toward her. He was a slender weed of a boy back then. He calmly lifted his face toward the sky and whistled low and long. Above him, the hawk hovered, then circled. Once, twice. Then it landed with an oddly delicate grace on Charlie's jacketed arm, talons curling then gripping tight. Its wings settled.

A dangerous thing, this bird. A heavy thing. Emma could see that now. A goshawk, Charlie told her now. That's what it was called. Even though it hadn't escaped, even though this boy had exerted some sort of magic control over it while she was still frozen with fear.

But Charlie didn't flinch. He wasn't even wearing that long glove—was it called a gauntlet? He knew how to be still, this boy, Emma thought. So unlike her father. How had she never noticed?

His eyes locked on to hers. There was a smudge of something on his cheek, but Emma barely noticed.

"Don't worry," he said. "I've got him. He knows I trust him. And he trusts me."

Had his father taught him to handle birds? Or was this quiet, perfect fearlessness just inside him, this knowing about birds? He was her age, but he seemed so much wiser, older. Mostly it was the way he said the word "trust." When her father described how he "trusted" Frank Ryan, the so-called family man, he sounded like an idiot. When Charlie said the word, it sounded as he'd carved it in stone at the very moment it flowed from his lips.

Something wonderful and fierce wrapped itself around Emma's heart at that moment. Charlie. The bird. The bright heat of the day. The tanned skin of Charlie's wrist as it peeked from his sleeve, the delicate grace of his bones, vulnerable to the hawk on his arm, yet somehow strong and secure. She stared at the goshawk's talons and imagined she could feel something like that deep inside, taking hold.

So strange. Emma had expected, and been disappointed by, and longed for so many things since moving here. But a boy had not been one of them.

Neither had getting punished, of course. By the time Emma returned home, Jamie and Lucy had eaten most of the chocolate cake, and her mother was shaking her head with a scowl as she wiped up the remaining crumbs. Had her mother gone to find Mr. Ryan? Emma never did find out.

After that, Florida seemed different. Less strange and awful. Or maybe it wasn't different at all. Maybe it was only that now instead of seeing a swampy, foreign place where life moved slower than she wanted, and her worries felt bigger than she was, Emma saw only Charlie.

THE SMOKE SMELL grew stronger and overpowering, as Emma and Charlie ran from the dock, the unmoored rowboat drifting back to sea behind them.

"Hurry," she gasped. She ripped the bottles from her pockets—they were useless now—and smashed them to the ground. "Oh my God, Charlie. Hurry."

But by the time they reached the museum, it was too late.

Someone had barred the doors to the reptile house from the outside. And jammed the lock on the inner office door. There were no windows. So when the building began to burn, there was no way out.

They were all gone, too: the Ryans and the O'Neills. The parents. The siblings. Even her youngest brother, baby Simon, still and always two. The gators were mostly alive, having slithered out of their cages into the observation pool. But everyone else was dead, except Emma and Charlie, because Emma had insisted he row to the island with her.

It's a funny thing to learn about a loophole in the immortality. If you drank the tea, no disease or poison would harm you. Your body wouldn't age. You would live forever . . . unless you died of *unnatural* causes. Like being burned to death. Or other horrible things Emma wasn't sure of yet. But an escape clause, so to speak. If escape meant being reduced to a charred, unrecognizable corpse.

And now *they* had to escape, because Glen Walters would soon realize that he hadn't murdered them all. Emma stared, numb with shock, grief, and fury, at the smoldering ruins of the office. She could imagine Walters's followers approaching fast, grim and angry, shouting as they swept in to finish the job, shouting the words that until now they'd only hissed in the direction of the O'Neills and the Ryans.

Unnatural. Abomination. Evil.

There was no time to think. No time to do anything but flee.

"Run!" Emma told Charlie.

"Run!" Charlie told Emma.

They ran. He was all she had left now, Charlie Ryan. Loving Charlie Ryan was like breathing, an involuntary motion that would last as long as she did—which was forever.

THE HORROR OF what had happened washed over Emma in wave after heavy wave, threatening to pull her under as they made their way north. At one point she even said, "We have to go back. We can't leave them like that." Then she bent and vomited, and Charlie pressed a sweaty hand to her sweaty neck, telling her it would be okay, which of course was a lie.

"We can't," she repeated. "Charlie, we can't."

But he urged her forward, sometimes dragging her when her feet refused to move, as though the grief and loss had sucked the life from her, too. Vaguely she registered the harshness with which he pulled her arm. "Damn it, Emma," he said, "just keep going."

Charlie never swore at her. But he was afraid and grieving as well.

What a fool she'd been with all those plans, so carefully engineered. While she was looking one way, the only way she ever looked—at Charlie—Glen Walters had taken everything and everyone she cared about. Burned it to bits. Burned *them*. She would gladly rip the immortality out of her and give it to him and his Church of Light. *Take it*, she would say. *You horrible bastard. You evil man.*

But she had Charlie. They were together. Somehow, they would survive. That's what Emma told herself over and over as the sun rose in the sky and the world kept on spinning. That's what she told herself as she understood—really *understood*—for the first time that the world didn't care about the people who lived and died in it. Her head filled with images of the bodies. Simon's baby-fine hair blackened with soot.

Charlie tugged her arm. "Stop," he said. Something in the roughness of his voice made her glance up, but his expression was unreadable.

They were at a fork in the road. How far had they gotten? Fifteen miles? Maybe twenty. Not enough.

They'd sneaked north past Fort Mose, skirting a marshy area, fleeing in the dark. She'd remembered some half-forgotten school lecture about freed black men and the Spanish, all jumbled up with Frank Ryan's stories about the Calusas in the steamy stew that was Florida. A farmer had given the two of them a ride for a few miles but they'd jumped off his wagon when he started asking too many questions. After that they'd avoided the main roads as much as they could, but now the sun was coming up, and underneath the terror, Emma could feel exhaustion lurking.

A few miles back, Charlie had changed their direction, muttering something about maybe hiding out for a while at Ponte Vedra and then taking more back roads toward Jacksonville. They could get a room in a local inn and then find the safest route from there.

"We should go back to New York," Emma suggested. "We could be safe there."

New York had been her original plan only yesterday morning when they had gone to that stupid island. They would get more of the plant and brew more of the tea, just in case the whole thing wore off, and be young and happy forever. That's what she wanted. In a big city, they could blend in. If someone noticed them, they could just move to another neighborhood. Another borough. Like those stupid, awful gators, she thought, only half-ironically. During hot weather, they'd dig holes in the mud and hide until things cooled down.

"Emma," Charlie snapped, "we're not safe *anywhere*. Don't you understand?"

She hadn't heard that tone before. Not from Charlie.

"Maybe Key West, then," she said, hearing her own sharp-toned desperation. "We could double back and get someone to sail us out there and then on to Cuba, maybe. They'd never think we would do that."

But he was right. And besides, wasn't the beach at Ponte Vedra one of the places Charlie's father had said Juan Ponce de León once sighted land? Maybe the stories mentioned a hiding place. Only they hadn't made it to Ponte Vedra. They were here—wherever *here* was—a clump of ramshackle wooden houses. From one of the rickety porches, a gaunt-faced woman in a dark muslin dress stared at them with too-curious interest.

Emma turned away, peering down the road to their left and then the one to their right. No signs marked any direction or destination. Neither seemed to go anywhere. The sun was warming the air to a thick simmer of dust and heat. Her heart felt like it was beating only because it didn't have a choice.

Every time they stopped, she saw her family's faces in her head. It couldn't have happened. They couldn't be gone. But they were. *Oh, God*, she thought, *I don't know what to do.*

Beads of sweat dotted Charlie's forehead. "Em," he said. He paused. His jaw twitched.

Her heart stuttered, hard, like something had stabbed it.

"Em. Emma. We need to . . . we need to split up. It's the only way we can be safe. We have to leave two trails, or they're going to track us down. I know . . ." He swallowed and set his jaw. "It's the only way, Emma."

Was he joking? That had to be it. She was exhausted, but they had to keep moving, and so he was telling her this awful joke to keep her going. Maybe even get her angry because she and Charlie squabbled like mad sometimes, but that was different. It wasn't like when her own parents argued; it never lasted long, and it always ended up in kissing . . . and so that must be it. Now he was trying to make her smile even though both their hearts were shattered.

He wasn't his father, who'd still sneaked glances at Emma's mother while he prattled on and on with his endless nonsense, right up until yesterday—was it only yesterday? And now Mr. Ryan and her mother and the others were all—

No. Charlie was good and solid, and he loved Emma. He had given her that crazy pocket watch. He had told her all the secrets of his true heart. When they walked together, his hand would slip protectively to the small of her back. When they finished each other's sentences, she would laugh, because how amazing was it to know someone so well you could see inside the other's head?

She tried to see inside Charlie's head now. He didn't mean for them to separate. How could he? He was just trying to protect her.

"Don't," she said, and managed to smile at him, holding his gaze even though she could see his eyes shifting this way and that. "I'll be fine, Charlie. I'm strong. You don't have to—we're together. We'll manage."

"Emma." He did look at her then. Her throat felt constricted, as though the thick air refused to flow to her lungs. "I mean it."

"You don't."

He was saying more words, but her ears buzzed, and she had to shake her head a few times to actually hear him.

"No," she said. "That's something your father would say. That's not you—" Her hand flew to her mouth. She shouldn't have mentioned his dead father. She shouldn't mention any of them; it was too much, too soon.

"It *is* me," Charlie said. "And you know I'm right." Already he was turning, walking away fast.

What? No. They were here at this crossroads because he really meant to leave her, to go one way and force her to go the other? No.

She ran after him, skirt flapping against her legs, clasping his arm until he faced her, searching his face for something, anything to prove the lie.

"You have to go the other way, Emma." Charlie wrenched his arm away, abrupt and cruel, like his words. Then he added, "I can't do this. Not with you."

She didn't understand what "this" was, except that it somehow meant *her. Them.* But how was that possible? They were together. He was all she had left. "I don't believe you."

He walked a few more paces. She followed, her shoes leaving smudgy prints in the dust.

This time when Charlie turned, his face was ghost white, and his gaze settled somewhere over her right shoulder.

"Em," he growled, "it's not just that. It's—you know it won't work. Being together, just you and me forever. It's like the hawks, you see? They can't be held to one place. When I tie their jesses so they can't fly away, it's not natural. I love you, Emma. But it would never be enough. Not when we have to hide because of what we are. Better to split up now when it will keep us both safe. There's nothing left for us, Emma. It's all gone. You know it's the right thing to do. The only thing. Even if you hate me for it."

She shook her head violently. "I can't hate you. Charlie, I—"

His nostrils flared. "I'm my father's son, Emma. I mean, really, what did you expect?"

She knew it was a lie. She *knew* it. Because this wasn't the authentic Charlie. This was an impostor. But he wasn't backing down, even as his voice broke. She thought she might cry, too.

Something awful wormed itself into her heart. What if he was right?

From the corner of her eye, she glimpsed the woman on the porch, still staring. Maybe they *did* need to split up. Maybe they *would* be safer. If the Church of Light came after her then at least Charlie would be safe. Or if they followed him . . . She couldn't think about that. No.

"We'll meet up somewhere, then," she said, to herself as much as to him. "In a few weeks. Just tell me where, and I'll find you."

He shook his head and started back down the road he had chosen.

"Charlie?"

But he kept walking. Emma could see how stiffly he held his back, as though forcing himself not to turn around. The panic inside her welled larger, swirling with the grief and confusion. Could she be wrong? Maybe she *had* been fooling herself to think she could be happy forever with him. And what did he see in her now besides this girl who had taken him away so he couldn't even try to save his family?

"Please, Charlie." Emma was crying now, tears having formed somehow even though she was hollow and dry. When he didn't answer, she turned in the opposite direction and started down the other road, forcing one foot in front of the other. She listened, half-expecting to hear him running after her. But all she heard were the buzzing of insects and the occasional squawk of a bird.

By the time she allowed herself a final glance over her shoulder, he was gone.

Had she been older, Emma might have understood that Charlie was telling her at least one truth. Having lost everything but the one person he treasured most, the *only* thing Charlie had left to live for was keeping her safe. He'd abandoned her in this godforsaken place to protect her. That much was real. This is what happened in the worst of times. People hurt one another, said awful things, even as they tried to be brave. Gave up what they loved in order to save it.

But Emma was *not* older. Wouldn't be, couldn't be. She had yet to learn that the hero and the lame-brained idiot often wore the same face. And by the time she figured it out, she would have gained a fuller and more colorful vocabulary to define both Charlie Ryan's behavior that horrible day and her own. She would have remembered some other, important things about goshawks. But she also would have learned that both she and Charlie were actually quite excellent at dropping out of sight.

By the time she realized that, she would also realize something else: the only thing she knew for sure—the only thing the girl who prized certainty could be absolutely certain of— was that she was alone.

Chapter Four

"Turn right in two miles," the GPS chirped.

Emma adjusted her sunglasses. The hangover was long gone but the day still seemed a little too bright. She tried not to think of Matt. That whole thing was best forgotten. It was time to focus on what mattered, on what could matter. A clue.

Elodie Callahan, age sixteen, had been found floating face down in a gated subdivision swimming pool. Elodie Callahan, who was supposed to come straight home after her youth group's holiday party, the next to last day of school.

No one remembered seeing her after the Secret Santa gift exchange. No one remembered a thing until she was naked and dead in a stranger's backyard. She hadn't drowned, though. She'd been poisoned.

Happy almost New Year, indeed.

"Keep right," the GPS lady announced.

She was a bossy thing. In Emma's weaker moments, the GPS lady reminded her of her own mother, who took a great delight—as Emma remembered it—in telling her daughter exactly what to do and how to do it. *Sit up straight. Smile. Don't smile. At least pretend you're listening.* But unlike her mother's view on what and was not ladylike behavior at any given time, the GPS was generally accurate, which Emma appreciated.

Her thoughts turned back to Elodie. Emma tapped a finger on the steering wheel. Cars had come a long way over the years. They'd probably go a long way more in the years to come, but a wrinkled ninety-year-old Elodie Callahan, tottering around at the turn of the twenty-second-century, would never know about that. Or about the sharp-as-a-needle, turquoise-colored Avanti Emma had driven for a few glorious months in the '60s. Emma was fond of a pretty car. And fast ones, too, which had surprised her. Her current used Volvo was depressingly utilitarian, a box with Swedish safety engineering.

But she wouldn't be able to tell Elodie any of that, either. Like Emma, Elodie was frozen in time, but with one crucial difference: she was no longer alive.

Someone had given her something to see if she would die. Same as the other girls. Yes, Emma had figured out the pattern, but she had yet to figure out how to stop it. How to keep dead girls from turning up. No one would be safe until she did. Including her, although she worried less about that these days than she used to.

They were still after her, the Church of Light. They would never stop, so long as they had their zealots. More than once since she'd landed in Dallas, Emma had pondered calling Pete. But she hadn't. He already knew more than it was safe for him to know. Better go it alone as long as she could.

WHEN THEY FIRST met, Detective Pete Mondragon asked, "This a vengeance gig for you?"

"Not exactly." It was not the truth but also not a lie.

Even then he knew better than to push her to elaborate. He knew when to keep his mouth shut. Besides, it had started as an accident—the investigating, that is. The poking and prodding of people and facts, the uncovering of stuff that wanted to stay hidden, like evil men with no obvious motive forcing poison down a teenage girl's throat. But it became something she was good at, something intimately personal, more than something that just passed the time.

Sometimes, a murder or a disappearance caught her eye for no other reason than a gnawing ache at the sheer senselessness of it all: this undefined despair that told her if she didn't investigate, no one else would. There were a lot of people out there—young, rootless girls in particular—whom the world saw as disposable. Or whom the world didn't see at all. Which was worse.

But Emma saw them. In those moments, investigating and solving crimes felt like penance—even when none had ever borne a connection to Glen Walters. She wondered if she would ever stop what he had unleashed. If you'd believed him back in 1913, his "church" had already been around for centuries. He claimed the faith traced its roots back to the Druids on one side of the Atlantic and the denizens of a lost Atlantis on the other.

In a word, bullshit.

The same type of bullshit that attracted people decade after decade, convinced it would make them safer or happier or righteous. They drank the poison Kool-Aid. They waited for aliens to whisk them off during the return of a comet. They holed up in compounds and bunkers. Or worse.

The problem was, some legends *weren't* bullshit. Like the one about the girl named Emma O'Neill who celebrated her

first seventeenth birthday six years before America granted
women the right to vote.

The sheaf of police reports on the front seat next to her
wasn't a product of faith, either. It was real, and it was tragic,
and it was very likely the Church of Light's doing. Bullshit
disguised as faith had a way of making reality very ugly.

Ironic that Glen Walters was decades gone himself, but
had become even more powerful somehow. Dead heroes were
like that. His followers might have been mortal, but collec-
tively, they were eternal, just like her. They'd put their faith
in his bullshit. They would sink into the background. Vanish
for a decade or two. Then she would breathe easier, thinking
it was over—only to discover again and again that it wasn't,
that it never would be, unless she found a way to stop it.

As the traffic slowed to a crawl once more, she wondered, not for the first time, if she could put an end to Glen
Walters's mission without having to sacrifice herself. She'd
considered that option once or twice over the years: just
taking an ad out in the paper, or later on the Internet, beg-
ging the Church of Light to come find her. It's me, Emma
O'Neill, you bastards!

Wouldn't *that* surprise the hell out them?

But she never would, and she knew it. She couldn't go the
way of her family or those poor innocent girls or even Glen
Walters until she found out what happened to Charlie. Best
to focus on the present, as always. *Someone* knew she was in
Dallas. *Someone* was leaving a trail of missing and poisoned
girls, trying to find one specific girl. Her. And unless she was
mistaken, it was the same group that had destroyed her family and Charlie's family, that had destroyed *them*, Charlie and
her, over a century ago.

"EXIT IN SIX hundred feet," the bossy GPS lady intoned. "Make a right at the intersection. The destination is on your left."

Her mother would have loved GPS. Emma almost smiled at the idea of her mother behind the wheel of a slick automobile with a back-up camera and Bluetooth. And with the smile came a wince, because part of Emma always squeezed in pain, the part that refused to forget or toughen up. Maura O'Neill had been dead and gone for almost a hundred years. But Emma's mother would have bitched—politely, but still— about Dallas traffic.

Emma exited. Checked for oncoming cars. Made her right turn. Dallas Fellowship was on her right; you couldn't miss the huge-gated entrance to its college-like campus. She checked the signage and followed the winding road to the flat-roofed building labeled YOUTH MINISTRIES, which sat under the shadow of both a row of pecan trees and the church itself, a building so sprawling that she had to step back to see it all at once.

Such a large and well-established church seemed a bit obvious for the folks who might have chased her here, but you just never knew. Hiding in plain sight was a strategy she knew better maybe than anyone else alive. The world was tricky that way.

Emma fluffed her bangs in the rearview mirror, then gave her expensively distressed jeans, silky tank top, and red cardigan with the three-quarter length sleeves a cursory check. Her shiny pink toenails peeked out from the open toes of her heeled booties. Unlike last night's pair, these did not have spots of taco grease. She adjusted her brown leather hobo bag over one shoulder. Matt from the bar would have observed that she looked like a high school girl.

Which was exactly what one of the other IDs she carried in

her wallet, the phony school ID, confirmed. A second driver's license nestled in the adjacent slot, also put her age as seventeen.

Like so much about her very long life, it was as true as it was untrue.

"I'M EMMA O'NEILL," she told the secretary in a shy voice. She held out her hand.

The woman—Melanie Creighton, according to the name-plate on her desk, looked up with a blank stare. Then her blue eyes widened. She took a sharp breath, an audible sound like the air being suddenly uncorked in a bottle.

Bingo, Emma thought. So she wasn't the only one to notice that the late Elodie Callahan bore a somewhat noticeable resemblance to Emma herself. Right track, then. But would it lead to anything?

Melanie blinked a few times. "Sorry," she said. "I—you look like . . ." She shook her head. "What did you say you were here for?"

"I'm Emma O'Neill," Emma repeated. She smiled brightly.

Melanie finally offered a limp hand, fingers drifting over Emma's, her palm waxy. Another lesson from Detective Pete Mondragon: *If they just bend a finger or two and don't actually shake your hand, don't trust 'em. 'Cause you can bet they don't trust you.* Recovered now—a quick recovery, Emma duly noted—Melanie peered over her reading glasses. "What can I do for you, Emma?"

Her smile seemed genuine. That was the thing about people: They were often more complicated than they appeared. And also much simpler.

If you're gonna spin 'em a story, Pete had taught her, *keep it simple. And at least partly true. The less you lie, the more they trust you.*

"I just moved here from Florida," Emma said. "My parents aren't into church, but I thought . . ." She paused long enough for Melanie's eyes to lock onto hers. "I want to join the youth group," she blurted when the silence verged on awkward, something she was good at making happen. You learned a lot about timing when you had a lot of time. "I heard from . . . well, the kids at school were talking. They really like the youth pastor here."

The tips of Melanie's ears turned pink. This could mean many things or nothing at all, maybe just the thrill of having her day broken up. Something encouraging in the wake of a tragic and frightening loss.

"Pastor Meehan isn't here. But I can give you the sign-up form, dear." Melanie spoke fast. She opened a desk drawer and extracted a piece of paper. "It's nothing official," she said, handing it to Emma. "Just your contact information. You just come to the events. You'll see. What school do you go to?"

Emma was prepared. "Heritage," she said. Elodie Callahan's school.

Melanie's mouth fell open. She quickly closed it and covered it with her hand.

"I started right before vacation," Emma went on, letting her voice waver as though she was unsure if this was a good thing or not. "But you know the last few days of school before Christmas . . ." She paused, looking down, then back up.

Melanie took the bait. Swallowed it whole. "Oh, honey, it's a fine school. Lots of good kids there. Madison Faw and Bailey Beal. Love those girls. And the boys, too. Barrett Jones—he's the quarterback on varsity this year. And I think Tyler Gentry goes to Heritage. My own two boys graduated from there. Andy's at UT now and Christian's up in

Denton. And . . ." She trailed off, biting her lip. Her gaze roved Emma's face.

"What?" Emma prompted. Then, "Oh," with her eyes going wide. "Did she go here? That girl, I mean. The one who . . ."

It had been all over the news the past few days. In fact, it had been the aforementioned Tyler Gentry whom Emma had followed to that bar last night; she instantly recognized the name. Tyler was fond of underage drinking and the occasional recreational pill or two. But a closer look—even before she'd been distracted by Coral and Hugo and Matt and that bottle of bourbon—had turned up no connections. Tyler Gentry had nothing to do with the Church of Light. She'd trailed him just to be certain, for the simple reason that certainty was harder and harder to come by.

Emma, too, could be both complicated and simple.

Still, she didn't have to fake the tears welling in her eyes. Sixteen-year-old-girls should not be murdered. Elodie Callahan should have been enjoying her Christmas break. She should have been with her family at an all-inclusive resort in the Bahamas, possibly parasailing or flirting with the wait staff, or at the very least sneaking rum drinks in coconuts up to her room. She should have had the luxury of going to college, of getting hangovers that didn't miraculously melt away, of making mistakes and maybe living in a crappy apartment with sloppy roommates and realizing that however bold it felt to buy a taco off the street, a bellyache was inevitable.

"Terrible thing," Melanie said gently. "But don't you worry." She fumbled in a drawer for a tissue and dabbed delicately at her eyes. "They'll catch whoever did it. They will. You've come to a good place, honey. We're glad to have you here."

At least the last sentence was probably true.

"Everyone loved Elodie," Melanie added.

Not everyone, thought Emma, but kept quiet. Another lesson from Pete: *Be patient. People hate silence. They'll fill it for you fast enough. All you have to do is be ready to listen.*

Melanie wanted to talk. And Emma wanted to listen. That's what she was here for, after all. She had all the time in the world to catch Elodie Callahan's killers.

A BEAUTIFUL SINGING voice—that was the first thing people always mentioned when they talked about Elodie. Even her friends. Also, she'd been inducted into the National Honor Society. But according to Melanie Creighton, she had "enough of a wild side to make her interesting." It *was* interesting; Allie Golden back in Albuquerque had been shy to the point of being antisocial, from what Emma had uncovered.

Hiding in plain sight.

Emma studied Melanie's face as she rambled on about silly pranks, like toilet-papering Barrett Jones's house the night after a big football game.

"The next day Elodie brought him a dozen chocolate cupcakes. Smart girl."

Melanie's expression shifted. "Her . . . poor aunt and uncle. Here they take her in after her folks were killed in a car accident in Orlando last year, and she'd been doing so well. She was like their own daughter. And now this. I don't think you ever get over losing a child. Or a parent either, when you're so young."

"No," said Emma. "You don't."

Her mind raced with this new set of facts: Elodie had been a transplant (like Allie), and her parents were dead (like Allie's). "So she was from Florida?"

Melanie nodded. "Oh, that's right. You said you were, too. What part?"

"St. Augustine originally. But we, um, moved around a lot."

In Emma's head, pieces of a puzzle edged together. Tentatively. Maybe. Because lots of people could have poisoned Elodie Callahan. Maybe even Tyler Gentry, although Emma doubted it. Maybe he'd gone overboard with a date-rape drug and panicked. People thought horrible thoughts, and occasionally those thoughts turned to deeds, and girls turned up dead. That's how the world worked. Certain parts of it, anyway. The sick parts, the parts Emma had seen again and again over the years.

Was the Church of Light involved? Maybe. Were they connected to this place of worship in some perverse way? Looking down at Melanie's sad face now, Emma couldn't bring herself to believe it. Melanie certainly didn't know if they were hiding in plain sight. But regardless of the perpetrator, the murder of Elodie Callahan was an undeniable fact, one that would be true and unchangeable forever, even if their resemblance and their Florida roots added up to nothing more than coincidence.

Emma's gut told her otherwise. She tried to listen to her gut, because unlike her brain, it was seldom mistaken. On the other hand, there *were* those tacos last night. But if she'd listened to her gut years ago, then maybe she and Charlie—

The thought was interrupted as Melanie Creighton stood and swept Emma into a teary hug. "Welcome to the Fellowship family!"

Chapter Five

The first time Emma kissed Charlie Ryan—really kissed him the way a girl kisses a boy she loves, and who loves her back—was on the night of her *real* seventeenth birthday, her first seventeenth birthday, the one that counted.

Both families had just sat down to a specialty of her mother's, vanilla cake with lemon filling. Emma was wearing the new skirt that showed off her shapely ankles and a blouse with a v-neckline her mother thought was scandalous. So did Emma. Not that she'd ever say such a thing out loud, but it made her want to wear the blouse every day. By that time, she had given up taking her mother's advice on most things.

Seven years had passed since the day of the hawk.

It was Saturday, a relatively cool February night, and the Alligator Farm had done good business. The tourist population swelled in the winters. Even the gators had seemed to enjoy themselves while on display. The O'Neills and the Ryans weren't rich, not yet, but tonight their coffers were full of admission fees. Emma had sold out of the alligator figurines and commemorative postcards in the gift shop by the entrance.

Now that they were closed and the tourists had all gone back to their hotels and rented cabins, it was just the O'Neills and the Ryans. Tonight they'd crowded into the O'Neill kitchen for roast chicken and potatoes and then the cake—all Emma's favorites. Well, everyone except Baby Simon, who toddled around the house and occasionally out the door like a miniature drunk. He was not quite two, his birthday still a month away at the end of March.

Emma had been surprised by Simon's arrival, but then they all had; Maura O'Neill was close to thirty-eight when she'd conceived. But one thing was for sure (and thank God for that): Simon was the spitting image of his daddy. Emma was grateful for something else, too. Ever since Simon had swelled up in her mother's belly, Frank Ryan had stopped leering at Maura O'Neill. Now Simon kept her mother so busy she barely had time to look up. Still, she always managed to hang on Frank Ryan's every word.

"A story!" Art O'Neill demanded as they shoveled dessert into their mouths. The grown-ups had consumed most of a bottle of Irish whiskey, too, reserved for this special occasion. "Let's have a good one, Frank. It's Emma's birthday, after all."

No matter the occasion, Charlie's father *always* told a story. And he always made a big point of starting every story with how he'd inherited his "gift of gab" from both sides of his family, as though everyone here in this kitchen might forget this fact if he didn't repeat himself a hundred times. As he told it (and told it and told it), the Ryan men hailed from County Mayo in the "auld sod" of Ireland—hearty farmers and fishermen and craftsmen, proud stock who had earned a living from the work of their hands. Proud of their stories, too. Or so Emma added in her head. *He* certainly was.

At night, his paternal ancestors would gather around peat fires and talk of fairy forts and Tír na nÓg, the land of the eternally young. On his mother's side, the Montoyas, a mix of Spanish and Indian blood, also spun fabulous yarns at night—Frank knew them all. There were tales of a Calusa woman who fell in love with a Spanish shipwreck survivor named Hernando de Escalante Fontenada. Of a Calusa city that sprang up and then disappeared. Of a Fountain of Youth and its exact location. The tales were passed down to the children who came after her, and their children and their children's children.

Frank's maternal grandmother, Ester, swore she was a direct descendant of Hernando de Escalante Fontenada, swore that every word of what she told him was true. She barely spoke any English, apparently. So Frank would always quote her affirming the truth: "*Es verdad.*"

Here Charlie's mom would always scoff, chiding her husband not to be ridiculous. Mrs. Ryan frequently scolded her husband when the others were around to hear. Emma liked that about her. But Charlie's dad would go on talking, even as Charlie shook his head, embarrassed.

"Fountain of Youth, my ass," was Art O'Neill's usual response, but he would laugh with the rest of them. "Do you ever see any of these folks? No. Whatever the truth is, it's dead and buried with them."

None of this made Emma want to kiss Charlie any less. Charlie was not his father, any more than Emma was her mother, and thank goodness for that. But Frank Ryan always seemed stumped by one particular detail. He didn't mention it much. Emma wondered if he'd add any details tonight in honor of her birthday. According to his grandmother, the secret of the location of this mysterious Fountain of Youth had been passed on only to Montoya girls. At some point, one of them bore only a son.

So the chain was broken. The family secret died. If there really were a Fountain of Youth, none of them would be finding it anytime soon. Emma hoped that this impossibility would one day make Charlie's father shut up. That hadn't happened yet, and she doubted it would happen any time soon. Certainly not tonight.

"ONCE UPON A time," Frank Ryan began, keeping his voice low and ominous, "there was a man named Juan Ponce de León."

Charlie edged his chair closer to Emma's. Under the table, his hand slid over hers. His skin was warm, and she felt a tingle. Across from them, Mrs. O'Neill stopped bouncing Simon on her lap and arched a brow. Emma pointedly ignored her. Charlie's fingers laced with hers.

"And King Ferdinand of Spain sent him on a mission," Frank was saying. The tale of Juan Ponce de León was one of his favorites, especially the parts that took place right here in St. Augustine. "It was a long and dangerous sea voyage. Juan Ponce de León was only thirty-eight years old."

Emma rolled her eyes. *Only* thirty-eight? That was ancient.

"No wonder he wanted the secret to youth," Emma muttered under her breath.

Charlie squeezed her hand. His thumb wandered to the center of her palm, making gentle circles.

She whispered in his ear, "If Grandma Ester was alive, she would die from boredom right now. You know it's true."

"*Es verdad*," she and Charlie both said at the same time.

Charlie bit his lip, trying not to laugh. He turned beet red.

"*Es verdad*," she breathed again in his ear, teasing.

"Shh," Charlie whispered furiously. But he leaned in. His soft earlobe met her lips.

Something in Emma's tummy went fizzy. He was a bold one underneath all his quiet, that Charlie Ryan. His father was still yammering away.

"Juan never found the fountain . . ."

This part of the story always made Emma sad. That a man would risk life and limb to travel across the ocean for something that he never achieved, never *could* achieve—because of course, what he was after didn't exist.

"Everyone thinks they know Juan Ponce de León. But they don't."

Emma straightened in her chair. This was new. Out of the corner of her eye, she saw Charlie's jaw tighten.

"Juan Ponce de León didn't find the fountain because he never planned on doing so."

"But wait, everyone says—" Emma began, and then shut her mouth as everyone turned to her, even Charlie. But it was true. Everyone *did* say that the whole reason Juan Ponce de León sailed to the New World—bringing the Ryans' supposed ancestor, Hernando de Escalante Fontenada, with him, only to get shipwrecked and wind up with the Calusa tribe—was to find the Fountain of Youth. That's why their families had a business! Tourists flocked in small clumps to the small, burbling stream by the river a few miles from the center of town. The huckster who ran it swore it was the real deal: the one Juan Ponce de León had discovered. People dipped cups in the water and everything.

Charlie's father waved a hand dismissively at her.

"It's the girl's birthday," her own father protested.

"The world remembers Juan Ponce de León for something

he *didn't* do," Frank Ryan said, suddenly speaking in his normal voice. "For a place he *didn't* visit. Yes, that's right. He never came here to St. Augustine. Not ever. That was King Ferdinand's dream, not his. You can't find a dream that isn't yours. You have to want it enough, and Juan didn't. He'd found the Gulf Stream, not that those royal bastards gave a damn."

Maura O'Neill narrowed her eyes at the salty language.

Emma frowned. "But the Fountain of Youth?" She couldn't help herself.

"It's here," Charlie's father concluded. "I know it is. I just have to figure out where."

"Careful, Frank." Emma's father laughed. "Wouldn't want a Calusa to put a poison arrow in your leg." This, they all knew, was how Juan Ponce de León had actually died. A poison arrow, care of the local Indians, the very ones that had supposedly spawned Frank Ryan down the ancestral line.

"Hell, they're my own people," Frank Ryan confirmed, and poured a glass of whiskey. "I'm not worried." He toasted the tribe that, according to his own legend of himself, had given him and Charlie their sharp, broad cheekbones. He held his glass high. "Here's to eternal life!"

He winked at Emma. She pretended she didn't see. Life—and the shortness of it, in particular—was no joke these days; there'd been a polio epidemic the previous summer. Lots of people had died. The threat still hung in the hot, humid air. It was like the smell of salt: always present, filling the adults' conversation when they thought the little ones weren't listening.

Now, his face flushed with more whiskey, Frank Ryan was smiling at Emma's mother, the way he had in the past. Even with little Simon bouncing on her knee.

Next to her, Charlie fidgeted, tapping his foot on the floor, looking peeved.

"Juan Ponce de León actually sailed here in a giant teacup," Emma whispered, trying to distract him.

But just as she was about to add, *"Es verdad,"* Charlie tightened his hand around hers.

"C'mon," he said. "They won't even notice we're gone."

She stayed in her seat—she hadn't even finished her cake yet—but he tugged her hand again and announced loudly, "Emma and I are going for a walk."

He said it as though daring someone to tell him no.

"Me, too," said Charlie's sister Katie.

"And me," said his brother Hugh.

"It's Emma's birthday," her sister Lucy added. Her brother Jamie was too busy eating cake.

"Just me and Emma," Charlie said, and then they were gone, and her life changed.

AT FIRST SHE figured he was going to show her something about the birds, because that's where his conversation usually went. And all this under-the-table hand-holding, and those words he whispered to her . . . well, if Charlie meant anything serious, he had yet to let her know.

"This way," Charlie said. He led her down the path under the trees, hand resting gently on the small of her back, the scent of the ocean and bougainvillea and their own sweaty skin mingling in the heavy air.

"I missed dessert," she said.

Not that she cared. It felt nice to be walking, to be alone with this boy, to be away from the suffocating commotion of so many people in one tiny kitchen. Charlie shrugged, so quick she barely saw, but said nothing. Instead, he guided her toward the dock that looked out on the tiny island where Emma's dad had found so many of the gators for the museum. He was so close she could feel his breath warm against her neck.

Now she couldn't even pretend to be annoyed anymore.

They slipped off their shoes and settled themselves on the edge of the dock, shoulder to shoulder, feet dangling over the side. She shivered, not from cold, but from the tingle of having him so close. She looked up, hoping he hadn't noticed.

He hadn't. The night was clear and the sky was studded with bright stars. It was the one thing she never tired of, this difference between the home in Brooklyn that was starting to fade from memory and the Florida swamp: the night sky was so clear and close it felt like you could fall right into space itself. No wonder Charlie was always looking toward the sky.

"That one's Orion," he said, pointing. She knew he was showing off but couldn't care less; she loved how he knew so much about the sky and its constellations. "And there"—he gently reached out and tilted her chin so she could follow his gaze—"Gemini. The twins. Half-brothers in the myth. Castor and Pollux. Remember that story, Emma?"

She did remember, particularly the part about Pollux, that he had been conceived when Zeus appeared to Leda in the form of a swan. Greek myths had always been a little hard to swallow—even more than the Fountain of Youth—but that one had struck her as more absurd than most. Why would people believe something like that? Then again, why would people believe *anything*, other than what they could know for certain?

"I do," she said.

He turned to her, his eyes glittering in the moonlight. "I

want to fly up there someday. And I'll be able to, I bet. Be able to go everywhere in this country and over to Europe, too. In aeroplanes and airships. It's already happening. Just like the birds. Imagine, Em. Just imagine!"

She shrugged, trying to focus on his words but distracted by his eyes, his lingering fingers on her face. "Maybe." She'd seen pictures of the Wright brothers' exhibition. She couldn't say that flying like a bird was something she wanted to try.

"Make a wish, Emma," Charlie said, letting go of her. He swept his hand across the swath of stars. "What do you want? I mean truly? Close your eyes and wish, Emma."

Hearing him say her name made her heart beat faster, the way those two simple syllables dropped from his lips. *Emma. Emma . . .* That fizziness in her belly surged. And then Charlie Ryan tucked a long finger under her chin, and dipping his head, kissed her full on the mouth.

"Mmmph," Emma said, trying, and failing to collect her thoughts—airplanes? Had they been talking about airplanes?

Her eyes fluttered open to see him, but he was so close, so immediate, so *much*, that she had to squeeze them shut again for fear she'd faint. His breath seemed part of hers, and oh! Was *this* what it was like? Kissing a boy, the right boy. *This* boy. Yes. *This. This.* He had been a part of her life every day since she was ten. Now she was seventeen, officially, and the entire world, *her* entire world, shifted. Until that moment, Emma had not understood all the possibilities of kissing. She had not understood *anything*.

His lips were warm and he tasted like lemon filling and mint.

"I love you," Charlie whispered in her ear. "Be mine, Emma. If you want to."

The way he said the words made her feel powerful and

giddy. His skin was hot and fragrant and musky. He nibbled her lower lip again and Emma wriggled and sighed.

"I want to," she said. "I love you, Charlie."

LATER—EMMA WASN'T SURE how much later—they were sitting on the dock, the stars above them. Her lips were tender from all the kissing, and her mind flying because he loved her. He had pressed his lips to hers, and now everything was different and Charlie said, "I have something for you, Em."

He slipped a small box from his pocket, his eyes firm on hers as he placed it in her hands.

"For me?" she said, and they both laughed.

Her fingers trembled just a little as she opened the box, pushing the lid with her thumbs. No wrapping paper or tissue, no bow, just a square black box. Her breath caught in her throat because no matter what was inside, this was the most perfect moment in her life, the most perfect she could imagine. Her fingers reached in and pushed aside the cotton batting to find what was underneath.

It was a pocket watch: gold case, held by a long gold chain, long enough to slip over her head like a necklace. On the front side, it was etched with a hawk in flight, wings spread wide, soaring toward an etched sun. Beneath the hawk, the print was so tiny she almost missed it, a series of numbers. 1706254.

"It's a serial number," Charlie explained as she ran her fingers over the bird and the numerals. "So you know it's authentic. Authenticity is important, Em."

She wondered if this was a dig at his father. But she nodded as though it was the most crucial of truths, as though a serial number was what made the gift so special—its authenticity.

"Look on the back," he said.

She flipped the watch over in her palm. Their names graced the back, also etched in the same delicate script: *Emma and Charlie*. Her fingers fumbled with the clasp, and then she found the secret, and the watch clicked and opened. The timepiece's face was white, with black roman numerals and two black hands, straight as arrows. And somehow—how had the watchmaker done it?—another hawk, tiny and graceful, drawn onto each hand.

It was beautiful. She should have said so.

Instead she said, "It's heavy," because it really was. She sensed it would weigh on her neck if she wore it, and wasn't that just like a boy, even *this* boy, to not realize the practicalities of the matter? Boys were practical in such different ways.

Charlie blinked. His lips turned down.

Oh, dear. She hadn't told him she *hated* it. How could she hate anything he gave her? But it *was* heavy. Was she not allowed to say the truth? Was that how it worked between them now? He had kissed her and so she had to just smile and not say all of what she was thinking? But no, she knew him better than that, because they thought the same things at the same time in the same way.

"It's the perfect weight for what it is," Charlie said. "I mean, Emma, look at it."

She looked. It was lovely. But it still weighed a ton. And that was fine.

His cheeks were flushed right up to the tips of his ears. Her eyes lingered on his lips, the ones that had kissed her until she was breathless and giddy.

"If you don't like it," Charlie began.

"I love it," Emma interrupted, because she did. So very much. But if she had designed it, then she would have taken into consideration—

The big hand clicked to twelve. From inside the heavy thing came the miraculous sound of rushing wind, making Emma feel as if she were flying high up, with Charlie next to her, and then faintly, the call of a hawk, so fierce that her arms and legs prickled with goosebumps.

"Oh!" Emma gasped. "Oh that's wonderful!"

Thankfully, Charlie's frown melted away. "There's a sound mechanism," he explained once the hawk had gone quiet. "At the hour and half hour. That's what makes it so special."

She nodded again. He took it from her, slipping it over her head. Against her skin the weight no longer bothered her; it felt as though Charlie had transferred a part of himself to it, a protective gesture, like when he placed his hand on the small of her back. *Authenticity.* She suddenly loved that word. Because that was Charlie. He was incapable of being dishonest.

"You really—?"

"Love it?" she finished at the same time, emotion welling in her throat. "Oh, Charlie. It's the most beautiful thing ever."

His smile was as bright as the stars in Gemini. He pulled her to him, holding her close, then closer, pressing his mouth to hers, and as she melted into his kiss, she imagined the watch keeping time with their thoughts and heartbeats.

Chapter Six

St. Augustine, Florida

1913

Not many days later, as Emma was remembering the feeling of Charlie's lips against her skin, his hands—oh, his hands!—she first heard the news. A traveling preacher had set up a tent revival just outside of town. Soon everyone was talking about Glen Walters.

He was "tall and silver-haired and fleet of tongue," or so Emma overhead at the gift shop. "A true wonder," one lady said. "An American treasure," said another.

When Emma brought it up at supper, her mother snapped at her. "We're Catholic. We don't believe in that kind of thing."

Emma almost felt like snapping back, *Then what* do *we believe in?* The last time they'd been to mass was years ago, back at St. Agnes in Brooklyn, where apparently she'd been baptized. She didn't remember that, of course; she'd been a baby. And at that last mass, Emma had been five years old; she remembered only the pungent incense and the life-size crucifix that hung from the ceiling: Jesus on chains, and those bloody nails in his hands and feet. She'd stare up most of the

time, wondering how much it had hurt. Faint fascination—
that's what she remembered about being Catholic. And now,
out of nowhere, it was important to her mother?

Emma wasn't even sure what a revival meeting was. She'd
rarely seen her mother so upset, nor had she seen the other
people around here so aflutter about things. Normally life—
and enthusiasm—moved so slowly here. But now she *had* to
find out what the fuss was all about.

Like kissing, she thought. And everything that came *after*
kissing. She knew about that—yes, she did!—though it was
probably best to keep religion and kissing separate in her
brain.

But Charlie would be at the tent revival. Maybe he would
look at her while this Glen Walters preached. Maybe Charlie
would hold her hand. Maybe they would sneak out again,
and he would kiss her some more. She would wear the pocket
watch he gave her even though it made her neck hurt because
it really was so very heavy.

"We won't be attending, Emma," her mother declared
firmly. But Emma's father had his own ideas about Glen Walters and the Church of Light.

"What we believe or don't believe is no one's business but
our own," he said at supper. "So if it's good for business to
be seen there like everyone else, why not?"

EMMA CRANED HER neck as Glen Walters strode up the wooden
steps to the stage, his hair as silver and perfect as the ladies
had said it would be, his skin weathered and tan, his eyes
bright blue. But when he stalked to the middle of the plat-
form, those eyes turned hard as slate.

Emma shifted on the bench, wedged tight between her
father on one side and Charlie on the other. Their families

stretched down the length of the row in either direction. Her skin was beading with sweat that dripped down her back. She already wanted to get up. Too many people. Too little room. Florida was so vast and empty, but she never remembered Brooklyn feeling so crowded, even though it was.

"Heaven is real!" Glen Walters cried, startling her enough to take a good look at him. Now those blue eyes had gone wild, lit with some internal fire. His voice boomed through the overheated night. "But you can't get there through good works alone. The Lord doesn't care about that. The Lord doesn't want sinners. But He forgives them."

The audience leaned forward. Her father muttered something ungentlemanly under his breath.

"Hush, Art," Mother whispered. "I *told* you we shouldn't have come."

"Man is a sinful creature," Glen Walters continued.

Someone to Emma's far right hollered, "Amen!"

Charlie linked his fingers through hers, and she gripped his hand like a lifeline.

Take me out of here, she silently begged him. *Take me out of here.*

The "tent" meeting wasn't in a tent, of course. Emma had stupidly expected happy things like the circus and cotton candy; she'd expected to feel seven years old again. Instead it felt like that last mass, but without the hanging Jesus. There was no ceiling because they were in the park. Every available bench had been crammed in front of the Church of Light's makeshift stage; almost every person in town was huddled here. The air felt more humid and thick than ever, an unwanted blanket she couldn't toss aside.

"Look around you, my brothers and sisters." Glen Walters's voice made Emma want to cup her hands over her ears.

Instead she held on to Charlie. "Look at the state of the world. We are moving fast toward hellfire. The faster we move, the more we forget ourselves. Trains. Automobiles. Airships. The telegraph. Are these things making us happier? Are they making us less sinful? No. They are making us covetous and evil.

"You've heard talk that the Church of Light traces its origins to the Druids. To Pagans. I tell you now, that this is true. But the Druids were the Lord's chosen until they turned from the right path and began building their mighty circles of stone, and the Lord destroyed them.

"You've heard talk that the Church of Light preaches of Atlantis. Of a shining civilization swept under the sea because they, too, believed that they were mightier than the Lord. And the Lord smote their glittering continent as he smote Sodom."

"Hogwash," scoffed Frank Ryan, loud enough that a couple in front of them turned around to stare.

Emma squirmed. She felt almost . . . naked, as though somehow everything she felt inside—even this new, private love for Charlie—was on display for all to see.

"He's an ass," Charlie whispered.

"Who?" Emma asked without thinking, and instantly regretted it. Charlie had never uttered a profanity in front of her. He'd probably been talking about Glen Walters, but there was always the possibility he was talking about his father. Charlie bit his lip, the way he always did when she made him laugh. His face turned red, and he squeezed her hand hard, shaking his head and smiling.

"Both," he gasped.

Now Emma was worried *she* might laugh.

Her mother shot them both a glare. Emma held her breath,

gripping Charlie's hand as tightly as she could, trying to focus on the sermon.

"Once again, in our time, Man wants to be God," Glen Walters told the crowd. "And once again, the Lord will strike us down for it. He already has."

He stepped to the very edge of the stage, spreading his arms wide as though he were about to take flight. Emma's stomach tightened. Why did he think they all needed to be struck down?

"The *Titanic*!" Walters hollered. "The greatest ship on earth. Unsinkable, they said. And where is it now, that glorious ocean liner? At the bottom of the ocean, keeping company with the carcasses of Atlantis. All that golden glitter rotting away. And why? Because *its* creators believed that they were God." He paused and lowered his voice. "Look among you, brothers and sisters. We shall cast out the sinners in our midst. Together we shall cleanse the community so the Lord won't have to do it for us. There is no way to heaven but faith. Remember this."

The audience rose to its feet and burst into applause.

Emma didn't stand. Neither did Charlie. He clung to her hand as tightly as she clung to his. She thought about those poor people on that doomed ocean liner. Was this man saying they deserved to die? That made no sense.

But the couple on the bench in front of them leaned forward as though pulled toward Walters by an imaginary string.

"He's wonderful," the woman whispered to her husband. "Just wonderful."

No, he's not, Emma felt like saying. *Don't you see he's just a charlatan?*

AFTER WALTERS FINISHED orating, there were tables of pie and cobbler and sweet lemonade, and almost everyone in town seemed happier and more talkative and more alive than Emma had ever seen. But she told herself that it didn't matter. Glen Walters and his Church of Light didn't have anything to do with her or her family. Besides, her parents didn't look happier. No, judging from the looks on her parents' faces, they wouldn't be going back to any of these "tent" revivals—good for business or not.

TWO DAYS LATER, when Emma was working her evening shift in the Alligator Farm and Museum gift shop—and thinking about Charlie (again and always)—a stranger burst through the door, smiling awkwardly as he almost tripped over the threshold.

He wasn't a tourist. He looked at her, for starters, not at the gator figurines and other cheap merchandize the tourists from up north ran their hands over but seldom bought. He was short and stubby. His face resembled a frog's—flat and wide and slightly bug-eyed. And he was sickly-seeming, shaky and coated with a thin film of perspiration. She backed away, even though she knew it was rude.

"Hello, my name is Kingsley Lloyd." He held out his squat hand, and when Emma took it—clammy and damp—he shook so hard that her elbow knocked against the counter. "I'm a herpetologist. I'm looking for Mr. O'Neill."

Emma tried not to make judgments—that, she'd learned, was definitely bad for business. "He's in his office," she said, gesturing behind her. In truth, her father was out by the gator house. One they'd named Horace had been acting sluggish the past few days. She wasn't even sure why she told this lie except that this man wasn't here to buy anything; that was obvious. But she couldn't leave him unattended in the store while she went to get her father, could she?

"You'll have to wait," she said. "I'm sure he'll be out in a minute."

At that moment, Charlie's father stormed through the door, his hair disheveled, his face smudgy, puffing air in his cheeks like he was ready to explode. "Damn gators," he muttered. "We've got all these shows scheduled and all these tickets sold, and now that one refuses to surface. Dug himself a hole, and that's that. Damn bastard reptile."

His eyes focused on Emma as though just realizing she was there. "Sorry, Emma. Have you seen your father?"

Well, now what was she supposed to say? To either of them?

The strange, frog-faced man approached Charlie's father and held out his hand.

"Kingsley Lloyd at your service," he said, and made a little bow. "It is your lucky day, sir. I happen to be an expert herpetologist. And I just so happen to be looking for employment."

Emma's mouth dropped a little. She had to remind herself that this was not ladylike, and snapped it shut. Part of her wished that Charlie would walk in, but another part of her wished he wouldn't because this would be a funny story to tell him.

"Herpetologist?" Charlie's father looked the man up and down.

"Worked all over the world," said Kingsley Lloyd. "Zoos and private collections and an alligator farm in Africa. Southern Rhodesia, near the Limpopo River."

Emma waited for Mr. Ryan to say, "Hogwash." Or something more colorful.

"Epidemic over there two years ago," Kingsley Lloyd continued. "Hit the gators' joints. All they wanted to do was hide and stay still. Stopped moving, and then a bunch of them up

and died. Healthy as horses, they were. Until they began ail-
ing. A type of reptile rheumatism. I learned all about it. Quite
the scientific mystery, you see."

Another charlatan, Emma thought.

Even Frank Ryan was sure to make the same judgment.

Instead, Charlie's father offered a huge, toothy smile. "It's
a miracle," he said. "You, sir, are a miracle! A herpetologist,
here to save our business. C'mon, then. We'll go find Art. Mr.
O'Neill, that is. We run this place together. He's going to be
bowled over that you dropped in just now. Amazing."

Mr. Lloyd glanced at Emma. "Thought he was in his
office," he said, but he was still smiling.

Charlie's father shook his head. "Nah," he said. "Art
never works in there unless he has to."

Emma felt her face flush. It didn't matter. Neither man
paid her any more notice. They were already out the door
like old friends.

Chapter Seven

Pete Mondragon answered his phone on the first ring.

"Emma O," he said, his voice deep and scratchy. "Knew you couldn't resist my charms forever."

"Forever's a long time," Emma said.

They were big on forever jokes. Pete was the only one who understood exactly how long Emma's forever really was, how the moment-to-moment would stretch into infinity while she stood still. At this particular moment, Emma *was* quite still—parked at the back end of the enormous IKEA parking lot, not far from the church.

She wasn't sure how much she planned on telling him. Her gaze wandered to a man in a striped shirt and baggy khakis. He loped by her, a wool beanie pulled low over his forehead. Five rolled-up rainbow-hued rugs poked from the top of the huge plastic bag slung over his shoulder. She'd probably been born at around the same time as the guy's great-great-grandfather. What would *that* man think of his descendant's rugs?

Pete cleared his throat. "Happy New Year, O'Neill."

She watched the guy with the rugs. "I think there's been another one," she said.

Pete appreciated when she got to the point.

He snorted. At least that's what it sounded like over the speaker. She pictured him on the other end—dark hair streaked with gray, forty-something. Thin ranging toward gaunt, which was hereditary, because the man loved to eat. Not that she didn't like food herself; she certainly did. Just that Pete consumed things with a level of enthusiasm that verged on animalistic.

When she'd first arrived in Albuquerque, she'd been investigating a string of girls who'd gone missing in and around New Mexico and Colorado. The kidnappings turned out to be the work of a religious fanatic, as she suspected, though not the Church of Light. The girls, thankfully, were all found alive at his survivalist compound down near Ruidoso.

Emma had ended up staying longer in Albuquerque by accident, really. She went on hard news and rumor, stirring the information until a piece of the puzzle fell into place. But her goals were always the same intertwined two: 1) Find the followers of Glen Walters, the hidden believers in the ever-evolving Church of Light, the killers who were after her—and figure out a way to stop them. 2) Find Charlie, if those same killers hadn't found him already.

The murdered girls resembled her, at least in passing, although sometimes she worked other cases for the money or just . . . because. Beyond that, it was an inexact science. A few lifetimes of inexact science. All of them hers.

And a new identity as a private investigator.

It hadn't been hard to fake the credentials necessary to get a license. All you needed was three years of "investigative experience," and she'd had decades, more than enough to allow her to ace the exam and the fingerprint training and even to forge her references and proof of previous employment. She'd gotten her most recent license the moment she'd arrived in New Mexico. Best to make everything official in case she had to end up with the local cops.

Then a girl named Allie Golden went missing.

She'd disappeared on her way home from school not long after the Ruidoso incident. She was about Emma's height with long brown hair and brown eyes. No one would take them as twins, but Emma saw herself in the high school yearbook picture of Allie—the ones on all the HAVE-YOU-SEEN-THIS-GIRL? posters. Enough to convince her that it had started up again, that people were tracking her, closing in, but uncertain of her exact identity.

The first time—that Emma knew of, anyway—had been a girl in Alabama, back in the '20s. Long dark hair. She'd been attacked by a mob and murdered, for no particular reason anyone could come up with. It stuck with Emma, that crime, the closeness of it, the coincidence. As did the ones that came after it.

She was being hunted.

So she investigated. Nosed around the pub in the bowling alley on 4th where Allie worked. Too young to serve the liquor, but she could wait tables. Lucky 66 the place was called. It had been anything but that for Allie.

"You a friend of the missing girl?" the cop had asked her the day she questioned the bartender. She'd seen him watching her out of the corner of her eye.

"Hired by the family," she lied quickly. She could tell he didn't believe her. But she pulled out her license, brazened it out. He looked worn out, this man, but focused. Brown eyes studying her, thumb rubbing across his stubbled chin. A brown trench coat, almost a duster. No wedding ring, but a faint pale line where one used to sit. A deep sandpaper voice, but firm, too. And a sadness behind those curious eyes.

Emma was more than familiar with sadness.

"Pete Mondragon," he'd said after a long, awkward pause.

"Emma O'Neill." She held out her hand. Inwardly, she winced. She hadn't used her actual name in longer than she could remember.

He was there the next place she went. And then the next.

She was working side by side with him before either of them realized that they were somehow, maybe partnering up.

Pete was as stumped as to what happened to Allie Golden as Emma was.

The search dragged out. One month. Two. Eventually, someone dumped Allie Golden in a field. The coroner said she'd been dead for less than a day. Poisoned. Something slow. Torturous. Then the murderers strangled her for good measure. All of which meant there had been two months in which Emma had failed to find her. Alive, that was.

She meant to walk away. To pull herself together and move on like always. But when the paperwork was all done and the books were closed on Allie Golden's unfortunate and unsolved murder, Emma let Pete Mondragon convince her to go out for green chile cheeseburgers at Blake's.

"They use Hatch chiles," he'd told her in a devotional tone. It verged on the mystical. "You know they have to actually register their authenticity with the state Department of Agriculture?"

"Oh?"

"Iconic," Pete said. "Mind-blowingly iconic, this burger."

Something about his adoration of a fast-food cheeseburger, his lonely and haunted eyes alight with the thought of those chiles, made her say yes.

Or maybe it was that he said the word "authenticity."

She'd only ever heard it used in conversation once before, in regards to a serial number that proved a certain heavy pocket watch was one-of-a-kind.

Pete ate three burgers to Emma's one. It was like watching the gators at the Alligator Farm snap their prey into a death roll. Another nugget of Pete Mondragon wisdom, imparted in between healthy bites of burger: *"Eat. Enjoy life. Otherwise this job will kill you. It may kill you anyway. Better go knowing you enjoyed yourself."*

Here he'd paused to wipe a glob of cheese off his angular chin, a glob he proceeded to eat.

In that moment, she'd decided to trust him. Not with everything. Not yet. That would come later. Eventually she would tell him who and what she really was. And eventually, he would believe her. But still, she'd told him enough that first night, over those authentic burgers. She'd told him that she *had* tried to enjoy herself.

That she'd loved a boy once, and he'd loved her. That he'd left her. And that nothing had been right since.

NOW, SITTING HERE in the enormous IKEA parking lot, she was being beckoned again by Pete's gravelly voice in her cell: "Tell me."

"You have the time?" she asked.

"Em, come on."

She told him what she knew about the late Elodie Callahan. That she'd been poisoned, like Allie Golden. When Emma finished, there was another pause, this one longer.

"You think it's connected?"

"Pete, come on."

"Had to ask. You working with the cops?"

"Not yet. I will eventually."

"You want me to take some time and come out there? I have days I haven't used."

The offer was tempting. But Emma knew better. The wise move would be for him to stay in New Mexico. If the Church of Light—whatever that even meant now, whatever they had metastasized into—had tracked her here, she didn't want Pete involved. She had not yet told him that all the dead girls looked like her. If he'd figured it out himself, which he probably had, he was choosing not to tell her. Knowing what she was and *really knowing* were two different things. She'd told him more since those early days, but not everything. *Everything* was dangerous.

"No, I'm good. I won't get in over my head." Emma held her breath, waiting for him to call her on her bullshit. She had been in over her head for more than a century.

"They identify the toxin that poisoned her?" he asked instead, his tone matter-of-fact.

"Something natural, hard to detect," she told him. "Reports also say she was strangled before they dumped her in the pool."

On the other end, a sniff. "Shit."

"Yeah," Emma said. "Bastards do what bastards do."

"So you think there's a pattern." More of a statement than a question.

"Yeah, I do." She thought of Coral—whom she had also not yet mentioned to Pete, because what if she was wrong about Coral's and her resemblance? And that reminded her of last night and Matt, and then she sighed again. Someday over drinks (not bourbon), she would fill Pete in on the rest of her notable lapses of judgment.

"Well," Pete said, drawing the word out.

She knew what he meant. Her instincts were probably right. Yet another Detective Mondragon rule: If it walks like a duck and quacks like a duck . . . They *were* hunting her again, the Church of Light, or whatever they might call themselves these days, just as she was once again hunting them. Only now they'd found a new way to force her out of the shadows. With the other girl, the one before Elodie, it might have been a coincidence. This was no coincidence.

Even if Elodie Callahan had been the same as Emma, if she'd somehow drunk from the same waters and was immortal, it wouldn't have mattered. She'd still be dead. They'd have burned her or dismembered her.

They would take what they wanted; maybe they had even found a way to extract immortality. Emma didn't doubt that possibility. But the autopsy report showed Elodie wasn't like Emma at all. She'd been poisoned, and she'd died.

"You sure you don't want me to come out there?" Mondragon asked again.

Just for one tiny, self-indulgent moment, Emma hesitated. "No," she said.

Better to keep him at a safe distance. Her mind was stuck on the image of Elodie Callahan and her thick, wavy brown hair and bright blue eyes. The thought stirred up a dim memory of something Charlie had said once, when he was holding Emma.

"You look like one of those paintings. The ones in that art book you have."

He'd meant the Pre-Raphaelite girls with the wild, wavy hair and creamy skin. Emma had known she was too much in motion ever to be that still and perfect. But Charlie rarely said anything he didn't mean. When he told her something, it counted.

Murdered Elodie Callahan would be quiet and still forever. It happened like that to girls who hadn't yet figured out just how impossibly evil the world could be. Maybe this wasn't the most modern of thoughts, Emma told herself, but it was true, nonetheless.

It happened to boys, too, of course. That's what had first given her a flicker of hope—the hope that Charlie was still out there somewhere, too.

EDDIE HIGGINS WAS the first dead boy's name. It was 1937, and Emma was in Chicago. She hadn't found Charlie, not even a trace of him. Two decades had passed since that last day on the road in Florida. She had searched all over the country—first across the south, to Louisiana, then northward, following the Mississippi—searched for that stubborn idiot boy, and she had hidden from the Church of Light, and now here she was, still alive and kicking and seventeen, and he was still gone.

It was time to move forward.

She told herself she wasn't giving up on Charlie, as much as she was being practical. She'd searched for longer than she'd been alive before *it* happened. Far longer than she'd even been in love. Maybe it was time to do the things that had been lost to her for so long. Charlie had been right, she supposed. Separating from him had wrecked her in more ways than she could count, but it had kept them safe. Or her, at least.

So she'd enrolled herself at Manley Senior High. A small indulgence as the world headed toward another war. A mistake in many ways, although it would save her just as her mistake in taking Charlie back to the island had saved her years ago.

Eddie Higgins's body was discovered early one morning in the middle of October, just as the weather turned crisp and the waves of Lake Michigan began slapping harder at the shore, hinting at the winter yet to come. He had been strangled and dumped on the steps of the monument at Logan Square, a tall marble column with an eagle on top.

It was all everyone could talk about for days.

"It's so awful," her classmate Sylvie Parsons said to her in civics the day after Eddie's body had been found. "Poor kid."

Emma understood awful things.

"Bastards do what bastards do," she'd responded, and Sylvie, who favored dark-red lipstick and bolero jackets over narrow-waist dresses and cursed loudly and creatively when she felt like it, shivered with delight and feigned shock.

Emma was—had been—in English class with Eddie. He was a senior at seventeen, handsome, slender, with dark, unruly hair. Her breath had caught in her throat the first day she walked into the classroom. Sitting there by the window, at first glance, he looked like Charlie. On closer inspection, he was taller, his nose was not as knife straight, and his skin was lighter and slightly pocked across the cheeks. And when he answered questions, his voice was higher-pitched. His thoughts were not particularly thoughtful.

And then he was dead, for no reason anyone could think of other than that horrible things sometimes happened, and this time a horrible thing had happened to a boy named Eddie Higgins. None of which would have been Emma's particular concern except for what happened as she and Sylvie parted ways by the library. Sylvie headed toward the science classes, disappearing around the corner just as a man approached. He wore a brown suit with wide shoulders and cuffed trousers, a dark fedora angled low on his head, and a visitor's badge pinned to his lapel.

"We're interviewing Eddie's classmates," he said, homing in on Emma. "I'm with the police. Can I ask you a few questions?"

Her heart had raced for a few beats. Then she'd told herself to calm down.

"You're Emma," the man in the suit said, scribbling something on a notepad. "Emma O'Neill, correct?"

Now her heart was thundering. Still, she kept her wits about her enough to study him and tried to remember every detail of his face—square jaw and light gray eyes and silver-streaked hair. He didn't look unusual or special, just the type of man who'd blend into a crowd.

"Did Eddie have any enemies?" he asked.

"I didn't really know him," Emma said, surprised that her voice sounded so even, so normal.

He asked some other things, but she wasn't listening. Instead, she was rapidly calculating how long it would take her to collect her things from the rooming house where she was staying and if there was anything there worth collecting at all.

"I have study hall now," she said. "Can I go?"

He nodded, and she walked off, past the library, and down the hall. Then she bolted around the corner and out a back door. Once outside, she broke into a panicked sprint. Because Emma had not registered at Manley Senior High School as Emma O'Neill. She had registered—in another frivolous but ultimately life-saving choice—as Emma Ryan.

Eddie's murder and his resemblance to Charlie had to be connected. They were hunting him, too. Which meant that unlike poor Eddie, he was still alive. Maybe. Probably. Hopefully. She wouldn't know, couldn't know, unless and until she saw him with her own eyes. Emma knew only this: they had found *her*. It would be a long while before she made that mistake again.

But a new Emma *did* surface. One who refused to mind her own business even if it put her in danger. Tragedy had given her fuller purpose, though it might take her a while (maybe forever) to understand what that purpose was. She'd learned something else, too: Even if people helped you, came on strong and kind, that didn't mean they weren't out for something, weren't looking to get around you, weren't perfectly willing to do to you—or to those you cared about—whatever they needed.

Like Glen Walters. Like his generations of followers.

Like Kingsley Lloyd, even. He'd wanted *something*. But what?

Funny, Kingsley Lloyd. She hadn't thought about *him* in any serious way for a long time. But he was, she knew, the one other person besides Charlie and her who could still be out there. Maybe. Doubtful. Very doubtful. Many times, over many years, she had told herself it was impossible.

Still, she had never stopped thinking that it really wasn't.

"PETE," EMMA HEARD herself say now, "could you do a background check for me on a guy named Kingsley Lloyd?"

On Pete's end there was silence. Did he even remember what she'd told him?

"That guy who told your father about the stream?" Pete said it almost indifferently, as though it were just an everyday thing to know someone who had drunk from a Fountain of Youth.

"That's the one," Emma said.

The world was getting smaller, had been for a while now.

Hard to fly under the radar when just a click of a mouse could unearth things that people barely remembered doing or saying. Kingsley Lloyd had disappeared long before that horrible last day in Florida. He wasn't anyone to her, not family, not a friend. Just the man who'd given them the tea and thus someone she held responsible for all that came after that. Thinking about him was therefore not something Emma liked to do.

But now she wondered. What type of man would lead people to a Fountain of Youth and not sip from it himself? She hadn't seen him drink that day in her family's kitchen, but that didn't mean he hadn't, did it? And if she was pondering this—far too late, but still, she had nothing *but* time—then wasn't it possible that Glen Walters and his followers and their descendants had pondered it, too?

And Charlie. If Charlie was out there—he *was* out there, alive, not dead, had to be—had *Charlie* wondered about Kingsley Lloyd? "He's a con man," Charlie had told her, "a charlatan, like you said. I don't want you around him." And she had bristled at him giving her orders because Charlie was not her father. But then they'd drunk that stupid tea from that stupid Fountain of Youth stream, and Lloyd had disappeared, and all of a sudden there were more dangerous things to worry about.

And then the danger came home to roost.

And then she'd been alone. And the years had passed as years do.

But what if—

"Em. Why are you researching a dead guy?"

Just barely, in the background, Emma thought she could hear him pecking in his signature two-fingered way on his laptop keys. Pete was quite the fan of the Interwebs.

Emma cleared her throat, taking her time about it. Around her, the back end of the IKEA parking lot was filling up. She blew out a breath. Immortality hadn't made her brilliant, but she had her moments, few and far between.

"I think Kingsley Lloyd might not be dead," she said finally.

Chapter Eight

St. Augustine, Florida

1913–1914

Emma was thinking about kissing Charlie—something she found herself doing most of the time when she wasn't actually kissing him—the moment everything in the universe changed again.

Shouting awoke her from her daydream—shouting about "purple flowers."

She was standing among the tomatoes and green beans and squash she was supposed to be tending. Kingsley Lloyd and Frank Ryan and her own father were running and whooping toward the house. She squinted at them. She knew they'd gone to the island to collect snakes and lizards; Kingsley Lloyd had suggested they start a new exhibit of smaller reptiles. Emma would always remember thinking in that instant, *Something must have happened, something serious.*

"Where's your mother?" her father gasped as the three men clattered through the gate. "Maura! Come outside!"

Emma glanced from one to the other. They'd returned too soon to have captured any new specimens, so why were they all in a tizzy? Even that ugly Mr. Lloyd, whom she tried to avoid as much as possible. She didn't trust the way his bulging eyes looked past people in conversation, fixed on some distant place. Or how he always seemed absolutely certain about *everything* he said. Emma liked to know things as much as the next person, but no one knew everything. She suspected that most of Mr. Lloyd's facts were as true as Frank Ryan's family stories. Not one bit.

"Look!" Her father waved a clump of purple flowers in his hand. Mr. Lloyd was clutching a basketful of the stuff in his skinny arms.

"Can you believe it?" Frank Ryan asked. He turned to Kingsley Lloyd. "You're a genius, sir. Brilliant!"

Emma's mother emerged from the house. "What in the Sam Hill is going on here?"

"We thought we might find some iguanas by the pond in the center of the island," her father said, talking a mile-a-minute. "You know how they love that pond."

Mother shrugged. Emma had been there only once, so briefly and so long ago now that she barely remembered. The island was not deemed safe for a girl. Charlie had been a few times, but he preferred the birds to the gators, mostly because his father preferred the opposite.

"Damn reptiles were hiding," Mr. Ryan cut in. "Couldn't find a single one. I told myself maybe we could capture a new gator instead, just so the trip wasn't a waste. And then we saw the stream. I swear I'd never noticed it before."

Here he rambled a bit—of course he did—about alligators and their territory and habits, and thankfully Emma's father stopped him before he launched into some tale of his Montoya ancestors and their gator-hunting abilities.

"It was growing right at the edge," Art O'Neill cried,

sounding triumphant. "Normally they only grow in the Caribbean. But here they were. Right here in Florida!"

He turned to Mr. Lloyd.

Turned out that when given his turn, Kingsley Lloyd was as long-winded as Charlie's father. More. Emma's attention drifted during most of it, but she caught the essence: Lloyd's grandmother was a natural healer. "Born poor," he said. "When you're born poor, you learn to make do. You pay attention to what's around you. 'Nature has everything we need,' she always told me. You just need to know where to look and what you're seeing.'"

It was a pretty neat trick, Emma realized: Like Mr. Ryan, Kingsley Lloyd swore by the advice of a woman long dead. That way no one could argue with him. Once you molded your long dead relatives' stories into fact, you could make anything sound true.

"Science is proving her right," Mr. Lloyd went on, his raspy voice booming with enthusiasm. "And if she was here, she would tell us that the quickest and best way to avoid contracting polio is to drink a brew made from these plants."

Emma rolled her eyes, but she could feel the fear of polio just the same as everyone else around here, feel it like you could feel the St. Augustine heat or smell the salt. And not just in Florida. The newspapers regularly reported cases all over, even back in Brooklyn. Epidemics they called it. There was no cure.

"So you see," Emma's father finished, "we're going to steep a tea from the ground leaves of the plant and drink it, and all of you—all of *us*—will be immune to getting sick. It's a miracle, I tell you."

By this time Charlie's mother had joined them. She exchanged a wary glance with Emma's mother. But Mr. Lloyd was grinning like he'd won a pot of gold. Did he think he could make money from this potion or whatever it was? She bet he did. How could her parents be so naïve?

"You're a good man, O'Neill," he said. Lloyd clapped his hands together, then gave them a little shake. "You, too, Ryan. Protecting your families."

Emma wondered what Charlie would have to say about this. She already knew what he thought of Mr. Kingsley Lloyd. The man was a con artist. A charlatan.

THE TEA SMELLED like flowers. Well, flowers mixed with mud and salt and something that left a sharp, dark bitterness in her throat just from sniffing the cup. She wouldn't have even called it "tea." It was more like the same homegrown medicine everyone else drank to save themselves from polio and other diseases. That's *exactly* what it was, in fact.

"Drink it all," her father told them. "Every drop."

Emma wrinkled her nose. At the stove, bow-legged Kingsley Lloyd stirred the muddy liquid before ladling it into each of the other cups with his squat, stubby-fingered hand. On the other side of the O'Neill's kitchen, clutching his own cup, Charlie waggled a brow at her. Then he cast his gaze swiftly toward Mr. Lloyd. He made a deep "er, er" sound in the back of his throat.

A *frog* sound. Emma giggled.

"*Es verdad,*" Charlie said in a low voice. She laughed, so hard she almost spilled her portion of the smelly stuff.

"What did you say?" Frank Ryan asked with a sour scowl.

"I was thinking of Great-Grandma Ester," Charlie said. "Did she have a family story about magical tea?"

At the stove, Kingsley Lloyd's mottled-looking face turned a dark shade of red. "It's not magic, boy," he said.

"It's science." But there was something in his tone that made Emma sure he was lying. Except what kind of lie was that?

"I'm not a boy," Charlie said. The teasing was gone from his voice.

"Charlie," his mother began.

Mr. Ryan cast a long, hard look at his oldest son. "No, you're not," he said. "You're a man. Start acting like one."

"I will," Charlie replied, strong and firm. "I'll make my own choices, too."

Emma held her breath. The laughter threatening to bubble inside her died down. She could feel her own father's eyes on her, probably her mother's too, but Emma kept her gaze on Charlie. His eyes locked on hers, and then he raised his cup to his lips.

Emma felt a smile creep across her own. She realized that he was not giving in. He was doing what he promised his father he would do. He was making a choice.

Charlie drank, downing the whole cup at once. She watched his Adam's apple bob as he swallowed. *Charlie*. Her Charlie. That kiss had reimagined her, reimagined both of them. She was his and he was hers, and she wanted him in ways she hadn't understood she could want. Every day there was some new revelation: He had a tiny freckle on the tip of his left earlobe she had never noticed before. If he hadn't shaved, if the sun hit his jaw just right, some of his dark stubble turned auburn. He was ticklish at his ankles, and if she wrapped her hand around one, he shivered and laughed.

Emma lifted her cup and drank the liquid to the dregs—not because her father had commanded, not because her parents had been walking about with pinched faces for days talking about sickness, more intensely since they'd heard that ridiculous message of doom from Preacher Walters—but because

Charlie Ryan had shown her that she, too, could still own the choice to obey.

MUCH LATER, AFTER everything had changed forever and there was nothing Emma could do but keep living, it occurred to her that Kingsley Lloyd had been the only of them she hadn't seen swallow the drink. Maybe he never thought the tea would work. Or maybe he was afraid it *would*. Maybe he waited for them to drink first because he already suspected what the plant was, what it could do to those who consumed it. Maybe he was in shock that he might have actually found the thing of legends.

On the other hand, it was entirely possible that Kingsley Lloyd did not have a clue what he'd actually found until after it was all done and they were stuck with it.

Either way, he was right about one thing. None of them contracted polio.

SIMON WAS THE first to catch their eyes.

1913 turned to 1914, but nobody understood yet that they were no longer aging, not any O'Neill or Ryan. The problem was that Simon O'Neill was two. He was a chubby little thing, toddling around in diapers, still waiting for his second molars to come in. And he'd been that same chubby little thing for almost a year, even though he was soon to turn three. He should have been growing. Maturing from toddler to little boy. Instead, he was *exactly, precisely* a two-year-old. Endlessly asking "why." Banging on his toy drum. Crying when he didn't get his way. Frozen in some perpetual state of miniature-drunk-man neediness.

"Every baby is different," Emma's mother said over and over.

Emma knew enough about authenticity at this point to know that Mother didn't believe her own words. Mother knew something was *very wrong*.

But no one would admit it.

Not until the day that Kingsley Lloyd, having just returned from the swamps on one of his herpetology expeditions, shambled into the Alligator Farm and Museum gift shop. Emma had been looking at Charlie's watch, but when she saw Lloyd staring at it, she snapped the case shut and jammed the heavy thing in her pocket. The pocket watch with its birds was between Charlie and her. Kingsley Lloyd did not need to know about it.

He leaned against the counter, studying Emma with his bug eyes. She couldn't put her finger on it, but he didn't look quite as sick as he'd looked before. He wasn't shaky or sweaty, although his skin was still pasty and his eyes rheumy. But looking almost imperceptibly healthier didn't make him any less peculiar. If anything, his gaze was more intense.

Was he going to ask for lemonade? He usually did, though why he insisted on drinking it here, which inevitably cleared the shop of costumers, was as much a mystery as anything else about him. There was just something about the careful, exacting way he stared at her—at everything and everyone, even more, she thought, since he convinced them to drink that tea—that made her skin crawl.

"Do you know that lobsters don't age?" he asked.

Emma stared at him. "Pardon me?"

"Well, technically, we can't figure out their age. They just seem to, um, get bigger. But not any older."

Emma managed a polite nod. Where was he going with this? There weren't any lobsters in the swamp. She knew what lobsters looked like, but she had never eaten one. She had never thought about them in any particular way. But she was not a stupid girl. She knew he was trying to tell her something, maybe teach her some sort of lesson. But what?

Kingsley Lloyd's broad mouth stretched in a lopsided smile. He shifted his gaze to the window. Simon was lumbering around outside in his white sailor suit, clinging to his mother's hand, mouth red and probably sticky from peppermint candy.

"People can be like that, I think," Lloyd said, looking back at Emma.

People. She tensed. For the first time ever, someone had spoken of . . . *it*. This thing that Emma kept feeling, this *thing* she feared was somehow keeping Simon from growing. This thing that neither her parents nor Charlie's would talk about. Emma's heart skipped a beat. She lowered her voice. "Are you saying we're like lobsters, Mr. Lloyd?"

He gave a brief laugh. "Perhaps I am. You're a clever girl, Emma."

Gooseflesh rose on Emma's arms, and the hairs on the back of her neck prickled.

Every day she looked into the mirror, and every day, the same girl stared back at her. But what, exactly, was she seeing? It was easier to pretend it wasn't happening. Or *not* happening.

"Have you ever heard of the Fountain of Youth?" Lloyd asked her suddenly.

Now it was Emma's turn to laugh. She almost answered, "Of course I've heard of it—every time Charlie's dad has too much whiskey." Lloyd had never joined them (thank goodness) for family dinners—not yet, at least. So she said instead, "You know Juan Ponce de León didn't ever find it."

She hoped that might send him on his way. She wanted

to end this conversation. Kingsley Lloyd didn't want lemonade, so what *did* he want? Emma wished Charlie would walk in, but he was putting the hawks and other birds through their paces for the tourists. For business. For family. For their families' survival.

"I know," said Lloyd. "In fact, I know that he never *wanted* to find it. He was a noble sort. But think, Miss O'Neill. Eternal life. An endless rebirth. Renders conception almost obsolete, no?"

Emma blushed at the word "conception." The heat on her skin made her think of Charlie and the way he . . . What would Charlie think about this man and whatever it was he was talking about? Did Charlie think that his own face was exactly the same? They hadn't talked about it, not ever. As though giving the fear words would break the spell of this wonderful thing between them. But sometimes when she looked at him, when she watched his brows pucker as *he* looked at her . . .

"We're mostly made of water, we humans," Lloyd went on. "Did you know that? That's the key." His voice rose. "The Knights Templar thought to drink from the Savior's chalice. The Druids saw eternal life in the Evergreen tree. Our Indian friends here . . . they've got their own ideas."

He leaned closer. His breath smelled herbal and strong, something oddly unpleasant. There was a splatter of something greasy on the collar of his white shirt. "Everyone wants to get back into the Garden," he said in a quiet rasp. "Make it last forever, you know. There's power in that. Big power. And we modern folk don't even believe the fountain exists."

Emma frowned. "Because it doesn't," she said.

Kingsley Lloyd withdrew and straightened himself. "You know better, my dear," he said. "But be careful. No one else knows. Not a single soul. Not even the ones who keep searching."

Emma's heart gave a sharp stutter.

"I needed to be sure. We scientists, that's how we work."

"Sure of what?"

He didn't answer. Instead he finally took the hint and left.

Grown-ups are crazy, Emma told herself. But the explanation felt as false as her mother's words about Simon.

THAT NIGHT OUT by the docks, Charlie whispered, "Emma, do you feel different?"

She was dizzy from his kisses, holding on to him as he stepped back. She'd been expecting him to say, "I love you." Or maybe, "I want you." Or possibly just take her hand and walk with her to the private little arbor a few feet away and lie in the grass, and she would let him slip his hands anywhere they wanted to go.

Emma had not yet contemplated the possibility of actually making love with him. But she sensed that someday she would like very much to be seduced by Charlie Ryan. She knew nice girls shouldn't think things like this. But secretly, Emma also sensed she wasn't all that nice.

"Yes," she said. Because at that moment, she thought he meant because of the kissing. She leaned into him, but he backed off again.

"I know how *that* makes you feel," he teased. Then his grin clouded over. He took her hands in his, pressing warmth into her. "I mean . . . something's happened, Em. Don't you feel . . . an energy?"

She *did* feel it. She closed her eyes. The thick, warm, salty air swirled around her. It was a perfume of the wildlife and the swamp and the ocean. When she opened her eyes, she knew exactly what Charlie meant, because she'd felt it, too. Not just an energy; she felt like energy *itself*, like she was a furnace or an engine or the sun.

Of course it was the immortality kicking in, not that she fully comprehended that yet, but still, she *knew*. It was spreading its magic through every vein, singing in her blood. The original Emma was being burned out, a new and permanent Emma rising from her own ashes.

On the other hand, girls who are kissed by boys who know how to kiss them always felt like that. She knew that by then.

Emma started to tell Charlie yes, she understood, that she sensed it, too.

But he let her go then and spread his arms wide, fingers reaching like he wanted to lift off the earth and fly. "I don't know what it is, exactly." She could see him searching for the right words. "It's like the earth is racing inside me. Like I could do anything. Be anything. Invincible." His gaze tipped again to the sky. "We'll go up there someday, Emma. You and me. We'll go everywhere."

Charlie wasn't normally this talkative. She'd always known this was what he wanted, to leave this place that was their parents' idea and embark on his own mad adventure. Emma wanted that, too, but mostly she wanted Charlie.

He edged his fingers slowly up her bare leg under her skirt.

"Oh," she said. "That tickles."

And then as his hand slid higher, she forgot what they were talking about at all.

Chapter Nine

By the end of 1914, well over a year since they had sipped from the stream, the difference she and Charlie had felt and shared became impossible to forget.

On New Year's Eve, Emma found her mother staring into the mirror and sobbing. They had finished scrubbing and sweeping, her mother's ritual. "You start the new year with a clean house," her mother always said at this time of year. "Then good luck will come your way."

Not this New Year's Eve. On December 31, 1914, her mother couldn't speak at all.

"It's going to be fine, Mama," Emma said. The words felt fraudulent even as they left her mouth. How absurd of her mother to shine things up as though it made a bit of difference.

Glen Walters and his Church of Light were hosting a New Year's Eve prayer meeting and celebration. Posters had been hung all over town.

FIGHT THE EVIL AMONG US
BRING BACK LIGHT IN THE NEW YEAR

Of course, the Church of Light had never approved of their families. They'd been unequivocal in their judgment. In their eyes—and words—the Alligator Farm and Museum gift shop was another symptom of general human decay in the form of silly pleasures and thrills. And their congregation was growing each day. Converts had taken solid root in this little part of St. Augustine. Maybe it was the heat that set their apocalyptic drums beating. Or just their inclination to find the devil in anything that felt different. The rumors had begun slowly and then with increasing speed and venom. Whatever was going on with the O'Neills and the Ryans went against the laws of nature.

Emma had never even been so much as disliked. Now she felt hatred, the same as she'd felt fear of polio, the same way she felt the heat of the sun. Hatred from the people who'd once been their neighbors, who'd spent time at the museum and the aviary.

THE FAMILIES HUDDLED together that night at the O'Neill's carefully cleaned house, toasting to 1915. The cheer was forced, the toasts were empty.

"They won't calm down, will they?" Emma's mother whispered.

"It can only last so long," her father soothed. "Things like this, they have a way of burning themselves out."

As for Frank Ryan, he used the word "immortal" for the first time. He said it apropos of nothing, during a long silence, but they all knew what he meant. He was referring to their collective condition, his voice awed and terrified at once. He wasn't even drunk.

Emma's mother—who no longer laughed at Frank's stories or hung on his every word—clutched at baby Simon.

"No," she keened, sobbing. "No."

"He won't ever catch polio," Emma's father said. (He *was* drunk.) As though this made up for Simon staying forever two. Emma's mother slapped him, hard, across the face.

"Mama!" Emma cried, shocked.

"Let her be," Charlie said, and he led her outside. They sat on the front steps. It was the first time Emma thought about running away. But where would they go?

"Are we?" she asked Charlie, barely believing what she was saying. "Are we really . . . *immortal*? Is that possible?"

Charlie was silent for a long time. Through the open window, she could hear her father and his arguing about what to do.

"They won't leave," she said. "You know they won't. The business . . . it's all they think about."

He didn't respond to that, but said instead, "I think we are. Em, I think something changed inside us. When I look in the mirror, I just . . . will it last, do you think? Maybe it's only—"

"Temporary," she finished for him. Neither of them smiled.

Emma studied Charlie's face. Did he feel exactly as she did? Because the truth was this: When Emma looked in the mirror, she saw that her eyes were wide and bright and clear. Her black hair fell in long waves. She was scared, but she was also thrilled, alive.

"We'll talk to Lloyd once the year turns," she heard her father say back inside the house. "We'll figure this thing out."

But 1914 turned to 1915, and Kingsley Lloyd didn't return to work. When Emma's father went looking for him at the rooming house where he lived, his landlady announced that he had "sneaked out like a damn thief" in the middle of the night. His room was empty. He'd left no note, no forwarding address, no real trace that he'd ever been there at all.

Emma thought, *He wanted to escape, too.*

ONE YEAR TURNED to two. And then two turned to three.

It was 1916 now. Three years since the Ryans and the O'Neills had drunk the tea brewed from the purple-flowered plant that grew on the island, at the edge of the stream Emma had never seen with her own eyes. Three years since the first time Emma and Charlie had turned seventeen.

They should have left. They should have run like Kingsley Lloyd.

"Talk'll die down," Art O'Neill promised his family again and again and again. Of course he did. Everything they had was tied into the business, into this place.

Early in January of 1916, a year after Kingsley Lloyd disappeared, Emma found herself hurrying down Main Street with Simon—headed to McClanahan's because Emma had promised her brother some candy and Mr. McClanahan always stocked sweets.

Simon still loved peppermints. He always would. She knew that now.

"Be careful," her mother warned.

But what could happen in broad daylight? Emma couldn't spend her life hiding, could she? The energy that burned inside her felt invulnerable, eternal. If what they thought was true, and it definitely hadn't been proven otherwise, then who could hurt them? She knew what she saw in the mirror every day. No, fear wasn't her problem. It was anger.

Preacher Glen Walters stood on the wooden porch of the mercantile, his silver hair shining in the sun—his *receding* hair. She saw it now: even in the few years since he'd arrived, he'd aged far more than her parents. His skin was perpetually red, lined, weathered from the sun. And the dark circles under his icy blue eyes had deepened.

He turned those eyes on Emma, then down to little Simon.

"How old are you, son?" he asked as they climbed the stairs, stooping to pat Simon on the head.

Emma tensed. It was a harmless tap. But she kept her eyes on that gnarled hand, the hand that balled into a fist and shook with righteous lies at the revivals every Sunday.

"He's four," Emma said through pursed lips. "He's small for his age. His birthday is in March." Which would make him almost five. Simon did not look almost five.

Simon smiled his baby smile. "Four," he repeated.

Glen Walters ruffled Simon's dark hair, fine as silk, wavy like Emma's, then curled his hand around her brother's skull. Emma yanked Simon away.

"Candy," her brother said and started to cry.

"I *know*," Glen Walters said softly, eyes tight on Emma's. "You think I don't, but I do. You can trust me, dear. Just tell me the truth." His voice was gentle, but his eyes burned with something not gentle at all.

"Let's go," Emma said to Simon. She dragged Simon back to the road. He was crying harder now.

"You shouldn't promise him something and then take it away," Glen Walters called after her. "Come back, and I'll buy the boy some candy."

"Leave us alone!" Emma shouted over Simon's shrieking. She picked him up and broke into a run.

"I can't leave you alone, Emma," Glen Walters said. "It's too late for that." His tone was polite, so different than his fiery fury at revival—but hearing him say her name like that was more terrifying than if he had shouted.

—

TWO DAYS LATER, Emma stood watching as Charlie tended to the hawks, tying jesses on their legs, fitting some with hoods, making sure everything was sturdy and proper. His hands moved steadily from task to task. When Charlie did something, he did it well.

"I wish we were them," she said. "Then we could fly away from here, and nothing could catch us."

"Em," Charlie began, then stopped. He straightened.

Glen Walters was strolling up to the aviary entrance. His dark suit—the one he always wore, even in this primeval heat—clung to his tall and lanky frame. He was sweating, but he had an easy saunter, as though he were a tourist or just an ordinary man out for an afternoon's walk. Except for his blue eyes. They were blazing.

"This is private property," Charlie said. He positioned himself in front of Emma. "Is there something you need?"

"Just paying a social call," Walters said. He removed a handkerchief from his pocket and wiped his brow. "Those are beautiful birds you have here."

"Yes, they are," Charlie said.

His voice was tight but firm, his posture straight and composed, and Emma could feel his muscles coiling.

She forced herself to be brave like Charlie. She said, "Bird shows are every afternoon on weekdays and Saturday."

Walters smiled. "Good to know," he said. "Though I wouldn't count on *every* afternoon."

Only when Walters had turned and walked slowly out of sight did Emma realize she was clutching Charlie's hand tight enough that all their fingers had gone white.

—

AFTER THAT, THINGS happened very fast, the way things do when the world is falling apart. The Church of Light organized a boycott on the Alligator Farm and Museum. And the people went along with them. Even the tourists—all those obscenely wealthy folks from the northeast who didn't believe in anything but money—stopped coming. Rumors spread that the alligators were poorly housed and dangerous. A THREAT TO THE COMMUNITY, read one newspaper editorial.

Then the museum was vandalized. At first just eggs thrown, like boys might do on All Hallows' Eve. Then rocks through the windows. Shattered glass. Then worse. The birds let loose from the aviary. Charlie's favorite goshawk, the very same one who'd landed on Charlie's arm that day Emma knew he was her love, was found dead.

They reported it all to the police, of course. But nothing was done. The town was watching. Fingers were pointing. Tongues were wagging. And through it all, Emma could see that no one in St. Augustine really knew what to do with a bona fide miracle except label it as an abomination. Nothing ruined the exclusive promise of eternal life, Emma learned, like finding out someone could get it and still remain in the here and now. Especially if you *weren't* that someone.

In February, shortly before Emma's birthday, Art O'Neill leaned forward at the dinner table—his face pale, his voice filled with emotion—and told his family that it would be time to leave soon.

"We need to get away from here. We need to make a plan. They'll never leave us alone."

Emma had already known that, even though it would be another few days before she witnessed Baby Simon guzzle that bottle of benzene, left on the table by their father after stripping the paint on an outside museum wall defaced by vandals with awful, damning words.

A FEW WEEKS later, Art O'Neill retained a lawyer—a fellow named Abner Dunn—who kept an office in a brownstone in Brooklyn. Together, they set up a trust for each of the O'Neill children. They were not hugely wealthy, but there was enough family money that had been kept aside for emergencies. Emma, his oldest, was named executor. She was the only one who knew. In the end, it wouldn't matter. She was the only one who survived.

"Something's bound to happen, Em," Art O'Neill told his oldest daughter. "I know I told your mother that it would all go away. But I . . ." Her father rested his hands firmly on her shoulders. His voice quavered, but only for a moment. "If it does," he went on, his gaze firm on hers, "promise me you'll contact Mr. Dunn."

At the time, Emma told herself he was wrong. That if she had Charlie, nothing bad could get to her. Not really. But she looked at her father and promised.

She had learned many things since her first seventeenth birthday three years ago. And one of them was this: Anything could happen. And sometimes it did.

Chapter Ten

Dallas, Texas

Three days after Emma's visit with Melanie Creighton at Dallas Fellowship—December 31, to be exact—the weather shifted again. Low gray clouds blanketed the sky. The air smelled like rain. It was almost twilight, not long to the new year. In the empty lot across the street, someone set off Black Cats, their sharp, repetitive pops filling the air.

Emma's tiny apartment was spotless: counters scrubbed, cabinets tidied, floors immaculate. Even the windows were freshly washed. She'd gone so far as to run the CLEAN cycle on the coffee maker. She had sorted every drawer, straightened the sparse items on the shelves in her closet, and wiped a soft cloth gently over the gold pocket watch that hung next to her bed.

Her mother would have been delighted at Emma's efforts. Her father wouldn't have noticed. But old traditions, well, what few had stuck with her stuck hard.

You start the new year with a clean house. Then good luck will come your way.

A hundred years ago, Emma had thought her mother a

fool. Now, she saw her mother's fastidiousness as an act of pride, a fist punching through the empty uncertainty of everything. Not that Emma believed in her mother's superstitious motive, in the good luck a clean-up would bring. The very opposite type of luck arrived at the O'Neill's doorstep. But the act itself had merit. It was tradition. It was control, or it tried to be.

Then again, Emma knew better than to try to control anything at all.

It would be getting dark soon. Emma sipped coffee on her tiny balcony, thinking about Kingsley Lloyd. So far, Pete's search had turned up nothing, but he had some other sources to mine. Apparently he knew "a guy" who worked Vice up in Santa Fe and could dig up Unabomber types—kooks and criminals who made it their life's work to stay off the grid. Her eyes wandered to her cell phone. She picked it up and called Pete.

"Got anything yet?" she asked.

"Nope. Em, he's probably dead. Why does this matter now?"

She bit her lip. "I didn't think it mattered. That he was alive, I mean. I didn't believe he was, not when I first met you. But then—"

"I get it," Pete said.

Emma made a face, glad he couldn't see. Luckily, neither of them was a fan of the video call. The whole point of the phone was not having to talk face-to-face, another belief she and Pete had in common. No doubt he'd made plenty of faces on his end, too.

"Okay," she said. "I *knew* he was probably alive. But it didn't seem important."

Pete grunted. He did this when he believed whoever he

was dealing with was not, perhaps, the brightest button in the box.

"Forever," Emma began, lapsing pointlessly into their familiar joke. "It's—"

"Yeah, I know. It's a long time," he finished for her. "But you're a PI, for God's sake, Em. I mean, you should *think* of yourself as one. You know better."

"I do *now*," she said. Which, for the most part, was true. "Bye, Pete. Happy New Year."

"You, too, Em. I'll spare you the New Year's jokes."

She picked up her coffee again, clutching it with both hands. She wasn't even sure why she was so hung up on Kingsley Lloyd now of all times, and here in Dallas, of all places. All she had to do was stand still. The bad stuff had a way of finding you, particularly if you kept putting yourself out there so you could find the boy you lost. Not that this was her fault, and not that Charlie himself hadn't been an ass in those last moments. But love interfered with "knowing better."

Screw Pete. At times like these, even given her expertise, she'd hardly call herself a "PI." She felt as phony as the credentials that had secured her license. A confused hundred-and-seventeen-year-old kid was more like it. She sensed that Pete knew better, too.

Her thoughts swirled gloomily. More Black Cats popping in the distance, another year was about to begin, and memories of Charlie Ryan creeping up: his wild brown hair, his capable hands, his ability to stay so very still. That was his magic, even before either of them had realized . . .

On the street below her she noticed a cop car cruising.

No siren, no flashing light, no reason for alarm. Still, it caught her eye.

Then another car appeared, careening around the corner. Her pulse quickened. She set her coffee down hard, liquid sloshing, drops scalding her hand. It was Hugo's ancient cherry-red Jetta—the '92 model, all boxy square lines and these funny round headlights that looked like hipster glasses. No one could forget Hugo Alvarez's car. Especially not Emma. She'd owned the same model car the year it had been brand new.

It screeched to a stop just out of her line of vision.

Coral Ballard's house.

Thoughts of Charlie faded.

Emma walked swiftly back inside, grabbing her keys and shoving her feet into her shoes, trying to stay calm but failing miserably. So she gave up calm and ran. She swiped to dial Coral's number on her phone as she raced down the stairs, not bothering with the elevator. No answer. Not even Coral's voice mail. Just ring after ring . . .

Emma shoved the phone into her pocket.

Hugo was standing outside Coral's house, agitated, his gaze focused on a wiry female cop in uniform. She wasn't much older than Hugo, her dark hair in a tight ponytail.

"Hugo!" Emma called, and he turned.

In that moment, he looked very young to her. He'd added a blond streak down the middle of his goatee and his oversized navy hoodie and baggy pants looked less like a fashion statement than an ineffective attempt to hide a thin frame. There were also intricate black-Sharpied faces drawn on his raggedy black-and-white Vans, for reasons she could only guess. In short, an adolescent boy, not yet a man. But Emma knew Coral saw these things differently than she did. Coral saw the boy she loved.

"Have you seen Coral?" Hugo asked her, his voice thick

with panic. "Her mom called because she didn't come home. She thought Coral was with me, but I haven't seen her all day. I figured she was getting ready for New Year's Eve or . . . I don't know. She's not answering her cell."

Emma shook her head. *It could be nothing*, she told herself. *Coral just lost track of time. That happens.*

Hugo was in motion now, pushing past the cop, or trying. She grabbed him by the collar.

"Hey, easy," the cop warned.

"I'm Coral's boyfriend," he snapped. "Has something happened?"

The cop glanced at Emma. Something had.

MISSING. RUNAWAY. KIDNAPPED. No one was sure.

First the cop hustled Hugo into the backseat of her patrol car for a little one-on-one. Emma hung back, hands in her pockets to keep them from shaking. Five minutes later, the cop shoved Hugo back out and screeched off, leaving him to pace back and forth on the sidewalk. He was a wreck—rambling, almost incoherent.

All anyone knew for certain, the cops included, was that Coral Ballard had left her house early that morning and not come home. She was not answering her phone. The GPS had been turned off. No one had heard from her.

"They think I had something to do with it," Hugo kept saying. "They think—"

"You *don't* have anything to do with it," Emma finally interrupted. She narrowed her gaze, more out of hope than suspicion. "Do you?"

Hugo froze on the sidewalk. His jaw tightened. "No. What the hell, Emma?"

"Had to ask," she said. "Were you two fighting? Did she

go somewhere? Off with her girlfriends, maybe? It's New Year's, Hugo. People get weirded out sometimes."

He stared at her. "You sound like a cop. Thought you were in school to be a nurse."

Emma briefly pondered possible responses to this. "I, um, well. I have friends who are cops. And detectives. And private investigators. Lot of nurses do."

It was dark out now. Someone was setting off fireworks again, more than just Black Cats. In the sky behind the trees, bright explosions of color flickered and vanished, leaving small, sparkling threads in their absence.

Hugo kept pacing. "Coral wouldn't run off without telling me. We're not fighting. We love each other. There's no one else. I'd know."

He's so young, she thought. *Too young.* But it wouldn't help Coral for Emma to remind Hugo that people wore masks, that you didn't know if someone was cheating, not really—not that she thought Coral would. Except people *did* cheat. The masks came off, and they said awful things and cheated and lied and kidnapped and tortured and killed. They demonized anything they considered "other," convincing themselves they were making the world a better place.

But Hugo's desperation to find Coral wasn't a mask. It was very real.

Which was bad news for all of them, Coral included.

Because that was it: confirmation that Coral's disappearance was connected to Emma herself. And to Elodie Callahan, and to Allie Golden, and ultimately to the perpetrators—to those who considered *her* the "other," who wanted *her* dead. Did they even know anymore why they wanted that? The image of Glen Walters with his gnarled hand on her brother Simon's head drifted up from the recesses of her memory, sharp and painful even a century later. People always said that time healed all wounds.

People said a lot of things. Believed an endless stream of bullshit.

"I'll help if I can," Emma said to Hugo now. "You just need to tell me everything you remember about the last week or so. Everywhere you and Coral went, everyone you remember meeting, even if it was only briefly. Anything you can think of. I know you probably told a bunch of this stuff to the cops. But now I need you to tell it to me, okay?"

His stare hardened. In part, she knew, because he suspected that her student nurse story was probably bullshit, too. But after a moment, he nodded.

"Okay."

"Good," Emma said. She glanced back toward her own apartment. They didn't have much time. If she were right about the kidnappings and the murders, it wouldn't take long. Just enough time to inject Coral with some poison and wait to see if it killed her. See if she was the girl they were looking for: seventeen years old with light, freckled skin, blue eyes and—at least in its original form—wavy, dark brown hair. And when they figured out that Coral was not Emma and therefore not immortal, they'd toss her body aside like garbage.

Or maybe they already had.

After all, unlike the others, Coral had grown up here in Dallas. Two keystrokes would bring up her class pictures and a million other bits of proof that she really was seventeen. She was not a foster child or an orphaned cousin or adopted with closed records. Which begged the question: Why take her in the first place? Especially when they'd already killed Elodie Callahan?

Emma's insides wobbled. She pressed her lips together in a fierce effort to stay in control.

Because they know I'm here. Because they're using her to make sure. They're using her as bait to draw me out.

"We'll find her," Hugo said. "Us or the cops."

The fear had seeped back into his voice. He was, she reminded herself, only nineteen. When Emma was nineteen, chronologically speaking, she was still living in Florida. Her family was still alive, and the magnitude of what they had become after drinking from that stream was only just sinking in.

"Yes," she told Hugo firmly, because the truth was a slippery thing and not always helpful. "We will."

Overhead through the canopy of trees, another celebratory firework lit up the night. In another few hours, it would be a new year.

It was time for this all to be over. More than time.

Hang on, Coral. I'll bring you back to him.

PETE CALLED AGAIN just before midnight. Still no leads on Kingsley Lloyd. If he was alive, he was clever.

"Yeah," Emma agreed. "I wouldn't doubt it."

She told him briefly about Coral. There was no point in keeping it quiet.

"I've got this," she said. She *didn't* have it. Not by a long shot. But what else was there to say?

"I'll come to Dallas," Pete said. "Just say the word."

Emma could tell by the sound of his voice that he knew there was more, knew she was selecting the bits and pieces she shared.

"No need," she said. She ended the call before he could say something else that might convince her to take him up on his offer. She would do this on her own. It was the only way.

After that, after Coral was safe and home and alive, she would use whatever Pete uncovered for her—his sources would find *something*, the tiniest of threads—and she would track down frog-faced Kingsley Lloyd. Then she would use whatever *he* knew to find a way to make sure the Church of Light would never come after her again.

And *then* she would figure out why that damn stream and those damn flowers had disappeared.

If they'd popped back up somewhere, she would find a way to destroy them.

And if she was still alive after all *that*—for the first time in a long while she fervently hoped she would be—she would find Charlie Ryan.

Chapter Eleven

New Orleans, Louisiana

1916

Four days after he left Emma, Charlie had made it to Macon, Georgia. He took rides where they were offered or where he could sneak them, walked when he couldn't. He figured Emma would cut north and then east once she made it out of Florida, probably heading eventually for New York like they had originally planned, so he moved west.

From Georgia, he wound his way toward New Orleans. He knew little about the city except that people said it was like Florida—a hot, humid, slow-boiling pot of everyone and everything. Something in that description drew him like a magnet. Or rather, he allowed himself to be drawn. He put one foot in front of the other, telling himself that it was all part of pulling Glen Walters and his sick followers off Emma's trail. He would force them to follow him.

"My name is Charlie Ryan," he said to everyone he met. "On the road from Florida. St. Augustine."

He burned through the little cash he had, getting drunk as often as possible. "Let me tell you a story," he announced loudly in some bar in Macon, banging his glass on the bar.

Then he launched into one of his father's old tales of Juan Ponce de León. It came as a shock to Charlie that, like his father, he could easily spin out a story. Maybe he hadn't been lying to Emma back at the crossroads. Maybe there was a kernel of truth there, that Charlie Ryan was more like Frank Ryan than he'd cared to admit. "He never meant to find the fountain," Charlie concluded. Then he added loudly and carelessly, "And neither did I."

The other patrons stared at him, some laughing. But he said it again because he needed to dig the trail deep and wide and make sure someone, anyone, would find him.

If they came after him, then his beautiful Emma might have a chance to escape.

He knew, even before the fire, that there would be no point in living without her. They had been each other's firsts, but he rarely thought about it in those terms. Emma was not a conquest. She was simply part of him. The part that had to go on living even after Glen Walters destroyed him. But she could do it. With enough time and distance, she could do anything.

Charlie was keeping her safe. Those ugly words he'd spoken to her back at that fork in the road . . . he didn't regret them. He'd worn that mask because it was the only way to get her to separate from him.

He didn't regret them.

He didn't . . .

By the time Charlie Ryan reached the outskirts of New Orleans—a city pungent with life and death and sex and food and liquor, the muddy odor of the Mississippi, and the briny whiff of the Gulf—he knew he was a liar. He'd made the worst possible mistake. He was not a hero, Charlie realized now, just a plain old fool. He'd lopped off the only part of himself worth saving: her.

Later, he would understand that this was the trouble with being forever seventeen: certainty. At the crossroads, he'd been absolutely certain he was doing the right thing. Now he was absolutely certain he had not.

He hated that he knew exactly how to word the lie. Bring up the hawks—exactly the weak spot to make Emma doubt what they had between them. But everyone was dead. What else could he do?

A million other things, *he realized.*

Idiot. Stupid, stupid, idiot. What if the Church of Light had tracked Emma? He would never forgive himself.

Charlie stood at the banks of the Mississippi, the wind blustering off the water and realized with that same absolute certainty that he had to go back. He had to go . . . where? He had no damn idea.

So he walked the streets of the city. At one point he lingered on the sidewalk and watched a funeral procession—a parade, really, some strange mixture of music and mourning and celebration. He thought of his family and Emma's. He forced himself not to wonder what had been done with their bodies. A dark-skinned woman in a colorful headdress offered to read his palm and sell him a love potion.

"No money," he said, tipping open one empty pocket. That much was true.

The next day, he found a job as a groundskeeper for the Old French Opera House at Toulouse and Bourbon Streets. The place had hit hard times, he could see. But it was still functioning. He knew his way around cleaning and gardening. And it could put money in his pockets.

"We took on some water during the hurricane last year," the manager told Charlie. "But we were lucky. Some of the houses uptown weren't so fortunate."

Charlie half-wished another storm would swirl in and pull him out to sea with it.

A FEW NIGHTS *later, after he finished up his rounds, he stood on the corner of Bourbon Street and waited for the cover of night—best to sneak back into the small room in the musty basement where he could catch a few hours' sleep. He had no money yet to rent a room anywhere; he was eating mostly leftover scraps from the performers' dressing rooms. Thieving this space was the best he could do for now. He would leave a few coins as compensation when he moved on.*

"You look hungry," a girl said to him, startling him out of his thoughts.

He recognized her; she was one of the seamstresses who came in to fit the costumes. He didn't know her name. Nor did he ask it. She was short and thick and dark-haired, an odd sprinkling of freckles running in a thin line from her jaw down her neck.

"I can make you something," she said.

He followed her to a boarding house off Canal.

When she kissed him, he kissed her back. Her mouth had a bitter taste, like stale coffee, but her breasts were large and full and pressed up against him, and her tongue was warm and insistent. He didn't stop her when she moved her hand down below his waist.

"You are a handsome one," she whispered.

She moaned against him, fumbling with the buttons on his fly. In that moment, he wanted nothing more than to lose himself in this girl whose name he didn't even know. Having lost the only person he would ever truly love, this seemed like proof of his betrayal.

Somehow the thought emerged anyway, the way thoughts

do sometimes when you need them the most. He found himself remembering the hawks.

You had to woo a hawk, had to be patient and gentle and know everything about it. You couldn't force matters, or it would fly away and it wouldn't come back.

Amateurs saw this as a flaw in the creature itself. That hawks were high-strung and temperamental. The amateurs forgot, or maybe they never learned that some hawks, like the goshawk Charlie had cherished, mated for life. They were headstrong birds who found the one they loved and never let go.

Charlie pulled away from the girl.

"Hey," she said, frowning.

"I'm sorry," he said. "I can't. I . . . there's someone. Someone I love."

She uttered a string of profanities, but he was already walking out the door. He was gone from New Orleans before morning. He didn't bother leaving a note at the opera house.

He backtracked all the way to Florida, traveling everywhere he thought she might go. But there was no Emma. Not anywhere he went.

The only thing Charlie knew for sure was that he loved Emma O'Neill, had never stopped loving her. She was his hawk as he was hers. But he had let her go, had in fact forced her to fly, and nothing would ever be the same until he found her again.

Always he waited for the Church of Light to catch up with him. Surely he had left an obvious trail. They would find him, and he would kill every last one of them, but only after he made sure that Emma was still safe.

But they didn't. Once, somewhere outside of Charlotte, North Carolina, he thought he saw a short, bowlegged man watching him from a corner. Kingsley Lloyd? But when he turned to look again, the man was gone.

A FEW MONTHS *later, Charlie boarded a ship for England. War was raging even if the Americans had yet to take the leap, and Charlie half hoped the Germans would blow the ship and his guilt right out of the water. But they didn't.*

And so, consumed with a dual desire to destroy everyone in his path and to lead astray those who wanted to destroy Emma, Charlie Ryan found a way to go to war.

Chapter Twelve

Dallas, Texas

The next morning, New Year's Day, the kidnapping of Coral Ballard—or "alleged kidnapping," as there was no actual proof—was all over the Dallas news. The day after that, it was trending online. By January 3, it had been replaced by stories on weight loss and gym membership, restaurants with heart-healthy menus, and an investigation into a local congressman's cocaine addiction.

Emma couldn't blame the media. Girls disappeared all the time.

None of the coverage mentioned Coral's friend, who had launched a full-scale investigation of her own. The media, of course, did not know Emma O'Neill existed. Or if it did, she was of no particular consequence. Which was how Emma liked to work. Off the grid, or making only the slightest of pings. If she was lucky, she'd find Coral before the Church of Light anticipated Emma's movements.

If.

No, she corrected herself. Not if. *When.* She would do this. She *had* to do this.

Since the news conference, a neighbor had come forward and reported hearing Hugo and Coral argue loudly about something. The media had attached themselves to the idea that Hugo, the boyfriend, was a viable suspect.

This made Emma simultaneously furious and wary. People always went for the easy answers. On the other hand, Pete Mondragon would have suspected Hugo, too.

Coral's parents appeared on TV, pleading for anyone who knew anything about their daughter's disappearance to come forward. Classmates taped up posters on light poles and stop signs.

Nothing.

The crazies had called, of course. Missing girls always brought out the crazies. The cops had followed up on as many leads as they could. After all, everyone remembered those girls who'd been held for years by that bastard in Cleveland.

This, Hugo informed Emma, gave the Ballards a strange sort of hope.

ON THE AFTERNOON of January 3, Emma returned to Dallas Fellowship.

Even after having been subject to the likes of Glen Walters, Emma wasn't opposed to the idea of a deity. But if God existed, He or She might very well be as perplexed about Emma's immortal condition as Emma was. And seemingly unavailable to help find Coral, although Emma was not one to rule out the impossible. *It's up to me*, she thought as she pulled back into the church parking lot for her appointment with the previously elusive Pastor Meehan.

Maybe there was something, even the tiniest coincidence or connection, in terms of the Elodie Callahan murder case that would help her find Coral.

It wouldn't be an obvious thing, she knew. As far as Emma had discovered, Glen Walters had personally and carefully trained his Church of Light followers. And they in turn had trained the ones who'd succeeded them over the years, on and on, for over a century. They'd grown skilled at hiding themselves in less overt trappings than a facility large enough to house its own Starbucks. In point of fact, they had lost their surface religious cover years ago. After that attack on the girl in Alabama—not that it had ever been directly linked to the fanatical disciples of Glen Walters by name—the Church of Light had not-so-mysteriously faded from the public forum. The tent revivals became less publicized and ultimately went the way of Prohibition and flapper dresses.

But their purpose, their focus, never seemed to waver. They hid now, but they wanted Emma dead like the others. That was their mission, passed on from fathers to sons, to grandchildren and great-grandchildren. (Were there women in their leadership, too? Who knew?) Emma would have found that intensity of purpose absurd if she hadn't lived through so many wars and conflicts. People held grudges for longer and killed for less. She knew it.

In a weird way, she sometimes found herself envious of the delicious false security that must come with thinking you know exactly how the world works. She hadn't felt *absolutely certain* of almost anything for longer than she could remember. Oh, she was positive she liked stylish cars and junk food and expensive shoes, not that she begrudged herself these too often. Positive that she'd been a shallow idiot once upon a time.

But her instincts made her wonder if she was even sure anymore what the Church of Light wanted with her. Maybe it was less her death (and Charlie's, because she refused to be anything but absolutely certain that he was alive) than the need for a symbol, something to hold their followers together. Emma O'Neill, eternal glue for the crazies.

And now, if her instincts were right, those fanatical disciples were hiding very close by.

And so, another trip to Dallas Fellowship.

"GOOD TO SEE you, Emma," Melanie Creighton told her as she entered the reception area.

Emma noted that this time, the secretary's smile did not reach her eyes.

Pastor Meehan believed they were going to chat about baptism. It was as good an excuse as any, although Emma Catherine Mary O'Neill had long ago been baptized one Sunday afternoon at St. Agnes Catholic Church on Fourth Avenue in Brooklyn. Of course, it might surprise the pastor to know that this particular church was no longer standing. It was a Whole Foods now.

Meehan stepped out of his office. He was a tall man with a shock of thick brown hair threaded with gray. He had a strong, square chin, bright blue eyes, and a slightly crooked nose, like maybe he'd been a boxer.

"You must be Emma," he said.

He ushered her inside, leaving the door open, and then gestured to two armchairs by the window. There was a small table between them. On it sat bowls of pretzels and ice, soft drink cans, and paper cups. He wanted her to feel comfortable. Or maybe this is what he did for all his guests.

Emma sat.

Pastor Meehan lowered himself into the chair across from her. "So," he said over the snacks, "what can I do for you, Emma?"

It was not the question she had expected. Not when she had rambled on about baptism and youth group T-shirts in her voice mail. Also of note: he didn't offer her anything. Not even a, *Help yourself, young lady*.

She held his gaze. In the outer office, she could hear Melanie Creighton talking animatedly to someone on the phone.

"I'm worried about what happened to Elodie Callahan," Emma said.

Pastor Meehan raised one nicely groomed brow. Then his eyes went sad. "Emma," he said slowly, his voice gentle. "What is this about? You're not a student at Heritage." Only then did he point to the bowl on the table between them. "Pretzel?"

If they spot you, Pete had taught her, *you have two choices: Keep up the lie or go for the truth.*

She contemplated the pretzels. "This was the last place she was seen alive."

Pastor Meehan leaned over the soda cans. Emma could smell something crisp and sweet on his breath. Peppermint. The scent reminded her, swiftly and viscerally, of Glen Walters and that day with her brother Simon at McClanahan's mercantile. *Silly,* she told herself. But her pulse jumped anyway and she struggled to hold Pastor Meehan's gaze.

Meehan's eyes softened. "I know," he said. "I think about it every day. Elodie was here, and then . . ." He raised that brow again, clearly waiting.

So you're a poker player, Emma thought. *Okay, then.*

"I'm a private investigator," she told him. Not the whole truth, but not a lie. "I'm sorry for the bit of fiction. We're never sure how cooperative people will be once they've talked to the cops. I'm sure you understand."

She unzipped her hobo bag and extracted her PI license. "I go undercover a lot," she said, which was also true.

Meehan was still leaning forward, pretending to debate which soda he wanted, hands cupping his knees. Out of the corner of her eye, Emma could see his fingers tense.

"And who, exactly, are you undercover for?"

"That's not something I can tell you," she said. "I'm sure you understand."

Meehan scratched his head, thick hair barely moving as he did so. Did he use product? She was pretty sure he must. Charlie had never used anything on his hair, that wild mess of hair she had loved so much.

Outside the open door, Mrs. Creighton was still jabbering to someone, punctuating everything with little whoops of laughter.

Meehan lowered his voice. "You're with the media, aren't you? You people come in here trying to dig up mud when a girl is dead? Shame on you, Emma. What do you think you're gonna find? If you want a reason for a tragedy, I suggest you look in the mirror. If you want me to pray with you, I can do that. I'd like to. But if you're looking for excuses as to why this girl was killed, I don't have anything for you. Evil doesn't discriminate. However old you really are, you look old enough to know that."

He really *was* a poker player. Or was he? The last part about her age threw her, she had to admit. It could have been intentional. But if he was bluffing, he was doing a good job of it. And there was another possibility, of course: Maybe he was *exactly* who he said he was. Maybe he'd taken off his mask to get rid of her because she'd taken off hers. If that were the case, she was half-tempted to hug him. Authenticity was a rare bird in this world, past or present.

"Fine, then," she said. "Just one more question: Are kids safe here?"

Meehan stood quickly. "Unless you have a warrant of some sort, we're done."

Emma swallowed and stood, too. Then she went for it. "Do you know a girl named Coral Ballard? She doesn't go here, I don't think. But I—"

"Coral Ballard?" he interrupted. A sharp, curious look crossed his face. "I saw her parents on the news. That's why you're really here? Then maybe I was right not to kick you out before you sat down." He hesitated, chewing his lower lip. "You look like a bright girl, Emma. Too bright to make assumptions. I'm the youth pastor. That's what I do. I also have an economics degree from SMU and ten years service in the Navy. Special Forces."

Emma fought to ignore his peppermint breath. He was probably telling the truth. It would be too easy to check. That she had not already looked into this was a failing on her part, not his.

Best to cut to the chase.

"I think Coral's still alive," Emma said. "I'm trying to find her."

"Isn't that what the police are doing?"

"They don't know everything."

Meehan's eyes narrowed. "True enough," he said, then walked to his desk, returning with a card. "My personal number."

He and Emma stared at each other for a few long beats. For a girl who hated making mistakes, the list of things she'd been off about over so many years was long and distinguished. Then again, she might *not* be off. He might be a lying bastard.

Still, she held out her hand and took the card. "Thank you."

He arched a brow. "Someone at a church didn't treat you right, Emma O'Neill. I would say that's my professional estimation."

It wasn't often anyone dug this close. Did he know about her? Was that possible? Or was she suddenly somehow that transparent? She thought about mentioning the name Kingsley Lloyd just to see how he reacted, but decided against it.

She shrugged. "That's not why I'm here." And that, too, was the truth.

"Another time, then," Meehan replied, escorting her to the door. "If you want to talk."

Chapter Thirteen

The nightmare was always the same. First Emma was talking to Charlie.

"There must be an antidote for it," he would say. "Some way to counteract, like for poison."

She would tell him, "No." And her heart would pound, and then she'd start smelling smoke, thick and acrid. They would row back from the island. But she would lose her shoes, and her feet became slick with coated mud. Every time, she slipped on the grass and fell heavily to her knees.

The dream shifted then to the museum. "Hurry!" she told Charlie. "Oh, God, Charlie. Hurry." The smoke assaulted her lungs. Flames had engulfed everything. In her dream, she ran faster, pulling ahead of Charlie, the heat of the fire drawing her forward in spite of her fear.

"Stop!" He grabbed her arm. "You can't."

She wrenched her arm away. Flames were shooting through the roof. From inside she heard one long, thin scream: her mother. She grabbed the door handle, and her hands blistered, though she couldn't feel the pain.

Her family was dead. "But they drank the tea," she would say over and over, willing their charred remains to return to life even as the horrible truth sank in.

Only this time the dream was different. This time, the smell of smoke didn't fade. Nor did the heat in her lungs. There was a shrill sound in the background, punctuated now by a pounding, a fist slamming against something over and over.

Emma's eyes fluttered open. She was coughing. She was awake.

The air reeked of smoke.

Now. Here. In her apartment. In Dallas.

"Shit," she said. "What?" She was on her couch, laptop open next to her. She'd been researching after talking to Meehan. She must have drifted off. So what was with the fire alarm? And the pounding—

Wait. Someone was at her door.

"Emma O'Neill!" a gruff voice shouted. "I know you're in there. Open up!"

She stumbled over to the door and threw it open. The knob wasn't hot; wasn't that a good sign? In her half-awake state, she saw Detective Pete Mondragon of Albuquerque, New Mexico, standing in her smoke-filled hallway. For a moment Emma thought she was still asleep. He wore jeans and the brown Carhartt fleece-lined jacket that always made him look like an aging cowboy.

"O'Neill," he barked, tapping the cement floor with his square-toed boot for emphasis. "Your place is on fire. Let's go."

Emma blinked a few times. *Pete? Why is Pete here?*

People were running up and down and she could hear sirens outside. The smoke stung her nose and eyes and tickled her throat, and she felt panic grow into something the size of a basketball in her chest.

Pete reached for her hand. "Emma, we need to go." He punctuated this with his own cough.

Emma stepped into the hallway, and her head swam suddenly. She nearly collapsed into Pete's arms.

"You are not going to freeze up on me, got it, O'Neill?" he grunted. He tightened his grip around her, nudging her back inside. With his free hand, he snagged her hobo bag from the narrow coffee table and waited until she took it from him. Then he nodded to the laptop. "You'll want that, too, O'Neill. So put it in that fancy purse of yours."

Emma frowned. "It's not—"

"Just do it."

She hefted up the laptop and slid it into her bag. It didn't quite fit, and something about this annoyed her enough to break through the fear. "Watch," she muttered, feeling like an idiot but nonetheless committed to what had just popped into her mind. She shoved the bag at Pete and strode the short distance to her bedroom.

"Wrong way, O'Neill."

She didn't answer. Her feet finally seemed to be working, so she dashed to the pocket watch, still resting on its hook on the wall by her bed. No way was she leaving without this. It was the one thing she couldn't lose, wouldn't lose. Not after all these years of hanging on to it—

"C'mon, sweetheart." Pete was at her elbow now. He had never called her "sweetheart," never called her anything that wasn't her name until this moment. "Did I mention that your building is burning? We need to get the hell out of here." His gaze skimmed the pocket watch as she jammed it into her bag. "Damn, O'Neill, really? You can't live without that? Looks like it weighs a ton."

"It's . . ." she began, but only ended up coughing more.

"Hell, Emma, it's from the boy. I know. No sense us both asphyxiating over it. Let's go." But his tone was gentle. Or as gentle as it could be.

The fire alarm was still screeching. Smoke from the hallway now filled Emma's apartment with a poisonous gray fog. The sirens outside were louder. She could hear a voice crackling over a loudspeaker, barking something distorted and incomprehensible, though she could guess the message: *Get the hell out of the building now.*

"Why are you here?" Emma choked out as she let Pete guide her out the door.

"Because you need me," Pete said. "And you're a stubborn cuss about saying so."

True enough. At present, Emma was in no position to argue with either of those observations.

"It's not your day to die, O'Neill," Pete added, and under his coughing, she thought she heard him chuckle. He put one big hand on her shoulder. "You think I wouldn't come for you? Then you got a screw loose, Emma O."

She stared at him. With a sharp yank, he tugged her down the hall, away from the heat. She'd been alone for too long, but even Emma O'Neill eventually recognized a lifeline in the dark when presented with one. After all, he'd thrown her one before.

Chapter Fourteen

Albuquerque, New Mexico

Four Years Prior to the Present

Allie Golden's murder turned up no connection to the Church of Light, no lead Emma might follow to the people who were hunting her. Random kidnapping, random poisoning, random everything. And so she had no intention of staying in Albuquerque. Not even after feeling at ease with Detective Pete Mondragon, not even after telling him that she'd loved a boy once, not even after the green chile cheeseburgers, though Pete was right: they were mind-blowingly iconic. Sublime, in fact.

She certainly had zero intention of sharing the rest of her strange and painful truths with him.

On the other hand, they'd investigated the murder of a young girl together. A gruesome and unfair murder. That kind of intense and tragic thing built bridges, wanted or not, even if such tragedies were the hallmark of your job.

Besides, Pete trusted her from the start, accepting at face value the Emma O'Neill she had initially presented to him. This was the Emma anyone could find with a cursory online search, the private investigator. If he'd looked deeper back then, he wouldn't have found much more, anyway, except that she never took on any clients and had zero client feedback.

She hadn't questioned his reason for believing her. Sometimes, she'd learned, it was like that between people. You just found yourself trusting them. Until you didn't. She could see that he was lonely, too, in that way you are when you spend too much time rooting around the dark underbelly of the world, when you see on a daily basis the kind of depraved horrors people are capable of. Maybe your own life has gone off the rails because of it, and you've brought yourself back, step by painful step.

That was Pete's story; Emma sensed it long before he told her any of the specifics.

Mostly she liked his company. He made her laugh with his clichéd advice, with those little hackneyed nuggets that always proved wiser and truer than most everything else she'd encountered over the last century. (A person's teeth really *were* the surest sign of privilege. Poor Allie Golden had terrible teeth. She'd never stood a chance, had she?) But Emma knew she couldn't stay in Albuquerque. If she did, it would be only a matter of time before he noticed the sameness she could never quite disguise, no matter how she changed her hair or wore her makeup or picked her outfits.

And if she told him?

Well, that was dangerous knowledge, and Emma had enough death on her conscience. Besides, how could she even start? Tell Pete that she had been born in 1896? That Benjamin Harrison had been president, and the first movie theater had yet to open? That not long after she turned seventeen, she drank a tea brewed from a stream that was in actuality a

Fountain of Youth? A fountain that had disappeared? Maybe for good, or maybe to spring up somewhere else? That people had been trying to kill her ever since?

No. Impossible.

Had it not been for the other secret—for what happened with a boy named Aaron Tinsley—she might not ever have told Pete the truth about her . . . condition. She would have stayed a few weeks, a month maybe because she enjoyed eating those cheeseburgers with him, and the pull of having a friend was strong. Having a friend was the first sign of having a life, a *real* life. But eventually, she'd have disappeared.

"I loved a boy. But now he's gone," she'd told Pete. That was enough.

Except it wasn't.

The truth was that Emma was already grieving when she'd shuffled onto the Allie Golden case. The truth, one she still could barely admit to herself, was that she'd suffered a loss— a loss beyond Charlie, one that had nothing and everything to do with him—and it had wrecked her in ways she thought she could no longer be wrecked.

It had been almost one hundred years since Emma had seen Charlie. Almost a century of keeping their secrets. Of wearing her seventeen-year-old face and everything that came with that.

In the end, she couldn't pinpoint the exact moment she knew she would tell Pete. Sometimes the truth is like that, sliding out and surprising you even as you're working up another lie.

THEY WERE HAVING lunch together at a diner on Candelaria. Emma knew it would be one of their last times together, knew she'd be leaving Albuquerque soon. It was a funky, tiny

ten-table place that served stuffed *sopapillas* and *carne ado-
vada*. The spicy *menudo* was Pete's favorite and the reason
he'd picked the restaurant.

"It's made with tripe," he explained when she sniffed at
the bowl. Emma had made a face. Tripe was just a nicer-
sounding word for "cow intestines." Really, tripe didn't
sound nice at all. It sounded exactly like what it was. There
were things she missed from the good old days. Consuming
tripe was not one of them.

"Best thing for a hangover," he added. "Not that I indulge
in those anymore."

She nodded. Watched him slurp a healthy chunk of tripe
and chew it with an admirable enthusiasm. He was the real
deal, Pete Mondragon. It was a shame she had to move on.

"Something on my face?" he said, and she shook her head,
realized she'd been staring. "You okay, then?" he added. He
leaned across the bowl of *menudo*, gaunt face shifting to a
solemn expression.

She saw in his eyes that he trusted her. She had given him
far too little, but whatever he saw . . .

She would tell him. Yes, she *was* going to tell him. She'd
tell him and then she'd go. It wouldn't matter if he believed
her or not. She'd be gone. But she'd have told *someone*. The
right someone. Suddenly that was all that mattered.

"There's something I have to tell you." She hesitated, the
words clogging her throat.

When she stayed silent, Pete put down his spoon. "I've seen
a lot of things in this job, O'Neill. Awful ones and wonderful ones. What people do to each other, what they are inside
where they think no one will ever get to. The part they think
no one will see. And here's what I believe. Whatever you are,
whatever you've been hiding, you're one of the good ones.

I'd stake my life on it. And I've never said that to anyone, not even my ex-wife." He let out a faraway laugh. "Which says something pretty bad about me."

Emma sighed. Was she really going to do this? He'd think she was crazy. "You're not going to believe me," she said.

"Tell me, anyway."

Something in those stark three words pushed her to say it. "I have this immunity in my blood," she began, thinking she'd keep it simple. But it wasn't simple, was it? So she told him all of it. Let him call her crazy. She was leaving. If there was one thing Emma had learned how to do well, it was that.

And so out the rest came. She told Pete about Florida and the stream and the plant and Glen Walters's Church of Light. About her family and the stranger named Kingsley Lloyd who had convinced Emma's and Charlie's fathers to brew the plant into a tea. About the fire that killed everyone she loved, except Charlie, the one she loved the most, or thought she did.

Confessing felt strange and daring and impossible. And despite what Pete had said, she waited for him to tell her she was insane. Because what else could he think?

But he'd *listened*. So she told him about Eddie Higgins who looked everything and nothing like Charlie Ryan.

By the time she was done, they had left the restaurant and were walking up Candelaria, Sandia Peak looming in the distance. There was snow at the top. She'd ridden the tram up once, a mile into the air, and as the car hung at the halfway point, she'd started crying because being above the world like that felt like flying, and that reminded her of Charlie.

"You ready to lock me up in some padded room yet?" she asked, only half-joking.

Pete looked pale and confused, but he shook his head. "Seventeen years old since 1913, huh?"

"Yup."

"From a plant on an island off Florida."

"That, too."

"And you're looking for Charlie and trying to keep one step ahead of whoever the big bad is now, yes?"

She nodded.

"And the PI gigs? I mean; you *are* a real PI I've seen you work. Hell, I've cribbed from you."

Emma shrugged. "Kind of goes with the territory, you know? Plus I've gotten good at it. The world's more connected than you think. One thing leads to another."

"Huh." Pete stopped walking. Trained his gaze on her. His eyes showed belief. If not in her story, at least in *her*.

"The boy you loved back then. Charlie. Was he good to you? Was he worth what you still feel?"

She didn't hesitate. "Yes."

As always when Emma talked about Charlie, she wondered what he was like now. What he was doing. What kind of man he was, even if he still wore a boy's face. And then came the crushing guilt of what was left to tell.

"There's more," she said. "From when I first moved here a year ago."

Pete didn't hesitate. "I'm listening," he said.

EMMA MET AARON Tinsley a month after she moved to Albuquerque. She'd dyed her brown hair red back in Portland, chopped off her waves for a close-cropped pixie cut. After all, her hair was the one aspect of her appearance that she could alter both dramatically and at will—and so she did so frequently.

The pixie cut, while not her best of choices, was also not a mistake.

Aaron Tinsley, however, was. He was a student at UNM. Twenty years old, eyes a mossy green and light brown hair that curled at the bottom of his neck. He smelled like soap and coffee and the clothes he'd just learned how to launder himself.

The first time Emma spotted him was at the coffee shop on Central, where she'd taken a job to get some quick cash. There was an ink stain on the tiny side callus of his middle finger, probably from a leaky pen. His boots were scuffed and old, and the collar of his plaid work shirt was frayed a bit on one edge. He sat for a long time at a table by the window, reading John Locke and scribbling notes in the margins. Before he closed the book, Emma saw that he'd highlighted *"Every man has property in his own person. This nobody has a right to, but himself."*

Emma didn't give a fig about John Locke except for a vague appreciation that at least the man hadn't considered women property—as solid a start as any to a political philosophy. Men she'd met over the decades, even in the twentieth century, weren't nearly as enlightened. And it had been many decades since Emma had last kissed Charlie. If she were an ordinary person, she'd be long dead. Instead, she was beautiful. Not even the awful hair dye could change that. Her skin was smooth, and under that red dye, her hair was the same lustrous brown it had always been. Her muscles were strong, her breasts firm, and her belly flat. Everything about her, physically, was still seventeen.

His gaze rose to her as she refilled his coffee. Something about those deep green eyes held her there, coffee pot still clutched in her hand.

It was an hour until closing, but the place was empty except for Emma, this boy, and Elias, the owner. Emma cleaned the tables and refilled sugar packets and stirrers and helped Elias hang *chile ristras* in the windows—because it was November, and Elias said the long strings of red pepper would make everything look festive.

How many places like this had she worked? How many kindly old men like Elias had she known? Most of them fathers with daughters of their own, shop owners and storekeepers who'd allowed her to scrape together enough cash to move on? Too many to count or try to count. Maybe she was feeling especially wistful that day. Philosophical, rather. Blame it on John Locke . . .

So she ended up talking to Aaron Tinsley, of course—Aaron who carried his cup and saucer to the counter and helped Emma with the last of the bright red *ristras* while Elias emptied the cream and milk pitchers. Outside, the wind had picked up and rattled the windows, but inside this tiny, warm space, everything felt safe.

"I love it when the wind blows," Emma said impulsively. "It feels like it could take me—"

"Anywhere," Aaron said, finishing her sentence.

Her heart squeezed. That hadn't happened since Charlie. Not once. She had been back and forth across the continent, looking for him wherever she thought he might go. Had even hunted pointlessly for an underground spring said to be somewhere below the Lincoln Center stop of the New York City subway system. (Emma never discounted these types of tales as apocryphal. New York City was just too full of secrets and urban hidey-holes and rats the size of medium-weight dogs to discount anything.) But in all of her searching, she found nothing. No fountain. No Charlie.

Over time, there'd been other boys. Not at first, but

eventually. Eternity was a lonely thing when your body was seventeen in every way but the chronological years.

EMMA PAUSED HERE in her story, not sure if she could or wanted to go on. Pete quirked a brief smile. "You think I'm judging you, O'Neill? I can't, and I won't. We're human. We love, and we screw, and we mess up, and we pick ourselves up and start over. If we're lucky, we do some good in the world along the way."

"Well, when you put it like that," Emma said. Then she told him the rest—up to a point. The whys of what she did, as best as she understood it. She didn't always understand the things she felt. She just felt them and tried to move forward.

"We closed up, and I walked out to the parking lot with Aaron," she said. "I kissed him, and he kissed me." She shook her head and fixed her gaze on the mountains. "I should have known better. I did know better. I should have driven back to my apartment and curled up on the couch."

"You went home with him," Pete said, and Emma nodded, eyes still safely on the Sandia peaks.

"I . . . it felt easier to just give up, you know? Tell myself that Charlie was dead. After all this time, I mean. Or if he wasn't then, why the hell not? He was the one who walked away first. Anyway, I'd move on soon, right? That's what I always had to do."

She paused, a lump forming in her throat, tears stinging her eyes. But she'd gone this far, so she might as well go all the way.

FOUR WEEKS LATER, just after New Year's Day, Emma realized she was pregnant.

Outside, the world kept turning. There was a light coating of frost on the ground and heavier snow on the mountaintop.

Aaron Tinsley had just moved to Santa Fe for an internship with one of the state senators.

Emma carried her secret around for another two months, hiding it and cradling it like all the rest of her secrets, noticing with detached fear and awe the subtle changes in her belly and breasts. She imagined it was Charlie's baby. A boy, she decided. He would be dark-haired, with tawny skin and when he got older, the high, etched cheekbones of his Calusa ancestors. Emma would tell him Frank Ryan's stories. She would make him giggle and teach him to say, *"es verdad,"* because of all the ironies, this *was* true.

"I was such an idiot," she said, and Pete shook his head.

"Not by half."

"I knew it was Aaron's, of course. I mean he was the only . . . oh hell, Pete. You know what I thought? I figured I'd already made up so much of my life as I'd been going along, why not this?"

Already she was pondering contingency plans. Because how to explain things when the child was seventeen, and so was she?

But it seemed a miracle somehow. A thing to conquer the emptiness. A person to love.

Until the miracle was gone.

She told him the rest: Ten weeks into her pregnancy, the living thing inside her simply was reabsorbed into her body. She felt it rather than knew, but an eventual visit to the doctor proved her correct. There was no baby. No sign that there ever had been one. Her stomach flattened; her breasts went back to normal. She was the same Emma O'Neill again—the same one she'd been and would always be.

That particular defining truth had never hurt so much as that cold March day, when she left the clinic in Albuquerque.

"I'm positive, miss," the doctor said on her way out. "The sonogram shows nothing. Is there a parent I can call to take you home?" He was matter-of-fact, cheerful, even. She realized he assumed she was young enough to be relieved.

There were many prices for her specific brand of immortality, and this was one of them. For the first time in all the years she had been alive, she wondered if Glen Walters and his followers were right in wanting to destroy her.

And now a new thought rose from deep inside Emma, dark and sad, one that changed her.

It was this: if any tiny particle of what kept her alive could bring back the baby that no longer curled inside her, she would gladly die to let it live.

She drove herself home from the doctor's office, alone as always. She cried a little, watching the sea of university students milling on Central, winding in and out of stores and restaurants—all young and vibrant, all smiling and laughing.

Everyone wanted to live forever. Everyone was sure they would.

THEY HAVE NO idea," Emma said to Pete when she was all finished. "What it's really like. To live forever."

"Most people don't," Pete gently agreed.

Emma rubbed her hands together, feeling the warmth of the friction. "I keep thinking I should want to be done. But I never am. I've stopped trying to understand that part of it. I mean, how selfish is that? To want to stay in the world all these years? Even if I never find Charlie. Even when it's painful. Even if I never get things right."

Pete shrugged. "It's human nature. We're survivalists above all."

It had not occurred to her.

Emma leaned back in her chair and smiled sadly at him. "Maybe I *am* just like everyone else."

It was the most honest thing she'd said in a very long time—before or since.

Chapter Fifteen

Dallas, Texas

The building management allowed Emma back into the apartment to get some clothes and whatever else she needed for the short term. Everything smelled vaguely like burned toast. Including her. The fire had started in the kitchen of a recently vacated unit down the hall, so it was very lucky that someone—Emma had yet to learn who—had smelled the smoke. It could have been a lot worse.

Management also informed the residents that it would be best if everyone found somewhere else to stay for the night until the smoke and water damage could be dealt with.

"Nice digs, by the way," Pete remarked. He elbowed open the glass doors in the lobby after collecting Emma's things. "Other than the barbecue vibe."

Emma harrumphed at him. It *was* a nice place. If you were here for eternity, you might as well be comfortable.

Pete didn't know, but she'd kept her promise to her father in those last days and looked into the trust fund he'd set up through his lawyer, Abner Dunn. And although it had taken Emma a while to give in, eventually the practicality of eating and living had gotten the better of her. Besides, Abner Dunn was the model of discretion. As had been the lawyers who had taken over his practice upon his retirement, and the lawyers who'd taken over after *their* retirement—generations of quiet, plainspoken, intelligent men and women, all of a type. Lawyers who believed she was her own daughter and then her own granddaughter and on like that. The current one was named Thatcher Elliott. He'd asked Emma to call him Thatch.

Human beings *were* survivalists. *Es verdad.*

And along the way, the sheer act of survival had woken in Emma an ingenuity she never could have imagined back in St. Augustine. It had also hardened her and made her a girl that the old Emma would have barely recognized, appearances aside.

This was the Emma O'Neill who hoisted herself into Pete's black Tundra. The survivalist. Now, with another hour gone and Coral still missing, Pete cranked the engine. The Tundra was a noisy beast. Outside, the clouds had returned, and the temperature had plummeted. Emma shivered. The air smelled like snow.

"I'm going to feed you," Pete said. "Because I can tell you haven't eaten. And you're going to fill me in. Pancakes okay with you?"

Emma thought of arguing, then thought better of it. Uptown Pancakes—its neon sign, a short stack with butter—sat a mile away on Lemmon. Even from inside Pete's ridiculously oversized truck, Emma imagined she could smell the bacon frying, mixing with the smoky odor of her hair in a not entirely unpleasant way. Her stomach growled.

Pancakes always reminded her of Charlie. Specifically: the first time that Maura O'Neill acknowledged that her daughter and Frank Ryan's son were more than good friends who'd grown up together. Not out loud. Like the immortality, it was a subject no one talked about, except to hint at. Certainly her parents had more important things to worry about than if their daughter had fallen in love. By that point, they had all been frozen in time together for going on two years.

But one Sunday morning, out of the blue, Emma's mother had invited Charlie to have breakfast with them. Emma knew why; Maura O'Neill had begun a fierce campaign of pretending that everything was normal. Asking Emma's "young man" to eat with them, formally, was part of it. Later, while they did the dishes, her mother whispered, "Charlie loves my pancakes."

Emma remembered her face flushing. Her mother's approval still meant something to her. And so she memorized the pancake recipe, a simple combination of flour and eggs, butter and milk. She remembered imagining the future: she would make pancakes for Charlie when they were married. And not just on Sundays. Every day if he wanted them.

Of course the future doesn't always work out the way you plan. Emma tried not to take this out on her love of pancakes.

PETE CLIMBED OUT of the truck and started across the lot. "O'Neill," he began, his voice quiet even though she trailed several feet behind, "how long did you think it would take me to figure out that these dead girls who keep popping up all look a lot like you? Including your friend Coral?"

Emma froze. She kept her eyes on the restaurant. Inside would be pancakes and bacon and a steaming cup of coffee. She *really* wanted a cup of coffee.

"Why didn't you tell me?" he demanded.

"*You* could have said something before taunting me with

pancakes," she muttered. "They make this sourdough batter one here that is seriously—"

"What else, Emma?" Using her name punched through her defenses; he rarely used her first name. Pete shot a wary glance around the parking lot and lowered his voice even more. "And remember that most likely, someone just tried to burn you alive. In case you hadn't noticed."

He had a point. She stepped forward, then paused again on the little walkway outside the glass door. "I . . . I needed to protect you. I couldn't . . . There's just a lot to it." She glanced around the parking lot now, too, gloomy under the dark clouds.

As if on cue, it started to rain—hard, stinging drops.

Pete made a disgruntled sound in the back of his throat. He ran his hand through his scruffy graying hair. Emma noted that he could use a haircut but thought better of saying so at this particular moment.

"Protect *me*?" he cried, his voice rising. He strode back to the truck, leaving her no choice but to follow. Then he gestured sharply. She followed him back into the truck, angry now, too, and also wet from the rain.

"Yeah," Emma said, climbing in and slamming the door behind her. Pete had no right to question her judgment. He wasn't her. He hadn't lived what she had. And then she thought, *Coral is missing. I need to find her. I need a lot of things, but right now, that's the most important one.*

The rain smacked the windshield, and Emma shook the water from her smoky hair.

"I didn't ask you to come to the rescue," she said. "You're not my . . ." *Father*, she had been about to say before she bit back the word.

Emma hated when she figured herself out. It made her feel

small and cranky. But the truth was still the truth: being friends with her was dangerous. She hadn't meant for Coral to become a friend. It was enough balancing Pete. Enough keeping *herself* alive and in the game. It would be so easy, she knew, to just run and hide. Not just from those who wished her gone, but from everything and everyone. Go someplace and just be. She could do that, couldn't she? Why the hell not?

Was that what Charlie had done? Was *that* the real reason she hadn't found him?

Maybe he was just better than she was at not being found. Of course he was.

Or she was just a shitty detective, which was also possible.

In her head, Charlie Ryan was still the Charlie Ryan she remembered, the Charlie from 1916. But why did she cling to that stupid lie? Over the years, she'd imagined different possibilities: Charlie would like football but maybe not soccer. He would enjoy texting but not phone calls. He would like thin-crust pizza, New York style, with sausage, and he'd fold his slice over and shovel it into his mouth. He would have owned the sleekest of automobiles over the years: A Dodge Charger because yes, Charlie would like muscle cars. Or maybe a Mustang. She wasn't sure what year. A Carmen Ghia. A 1957 Thunderbird.

And he would have learned to fly. She had dug into war records once and found various Charlie Ryans with service records, some who were pilots, but tracking them down always led to dead ends. She supposed he'd used aliases. Certainly she had, although she'd gotten sloppy about that lately, and look how that had turned out.

Because for one wrongheaded second she had thought she could have a real friend. Be a normal person.

And so people were dead. Again. And Coral was missing.

"From the beginning," Pete said, and Emma refocused. "Whatever you've been holding back." Then more quietly, "I can't help you if I don't know. So enough with the thickheadedness."

Her brows furrowed. "I am not—"

"O'Neill."

Emma's eyes stung now and not from the smoke. "I have to find her," she said. "Jesus, Pete. I don't know—"

"From the beginning," he repeated and touched a hand to her shoulder. "Repeat yourself. I don't give a shit. I have all the time in the world. Bad joke. But bear with me. I need you to fill in the dots." He shimmied out of his jacket. "And put this on before you freeze to death."

Emma almost smiled. "Don't think that's possible," she said. "But thanks."

She let him drape his jacket over her. The weight felt comforting. It reminded her of being tucked into bed. Or maybe it didn't remind her. Could she remember that feeling as viscerally as she believed she remembered, a century later? There was so much she didn't know. But Pete Mondragon, this strange protector, deserved to know as much as she did.

So she told him.

She told him what the Church of Light wanted, or what she believed they wanted: to find and destroy her and Charlie.

She did not say Charlie might already be dead. She would never say that.

"Or they want what I am," Emma clarified. "At this point, it's a toss-up. I mean it started as a witch hunt, you know that. But over time, well, things change. It's like you and I have talked about before. Everyone thinks they want to live forever. Until they do." She laughed sadly. "Not that any of them figured that part out yet. At least, I don't think so. Except for Kingsley Lloyd. If he's still alive, he's somehow the key to this whole thing, even if he doesn't know it. It's about power. Maybe they got to him. Maybe not."

"What else?" Pete pressed.

Emma told him everything else she could think of, everything about the death of Elodie Callahan and her visit to Dallas Fellowship and Pastor Meehan, laying it all out.

"I don't think Meehan's connected," she finished. "But I've been wrong before." *Too many times*, she thought.

By the time Emma finished talking, the rain had turned to soft flakes of snow. She'd never seen snow in Dallas before, although she knew it snowed here. There were still firsts, even after 120 years. She waited for Pete to tell her that she was wrong for waiting so long to bring him fully into the case, in trying to protect him, to keep him distanced.

But he said only, "And I know that you think Charlie is still out there, too."

She nodded.

"You know this is still all hard for me to believe, right?" Pete asked. He tapped his fingers on the steering wheel. "If you didn't look the way you look . . ."

"I know," Emma said, her eyes on the rain. "But I *do* look the way I look. And you don't. You look like you've aged since I last saw you, four years ago. You're grayer. The bags under your eyes are darker."

"Guess you don't learn manners living forever, either," he grumbled. He cleared his throat. "So you think this Church of Light—whoever's in charge at this point—is killing off girls to either find you or lure you out."

"Yes," Emma said. "I've studied the autopsy reports. That's

why it's been poison, because poison can't affect me. When they start to show symptoms, then the Church of Light knows it's not me, so they get killed. The Church of Light can't let them live."

Pete nodded. "So she might be dead, then?" He hesitated. "Your friend Coral?"

Something fierce lit inside her. "She's not," Emma said. "I'd know if she was. This time they know they're close. She's bait."

"So you're psychic now, too?" His tone was half sarcasm, half possibility.

That was the cop in him, she knew. You needed to be a cynic to survive in his line of work. She got that.

"Sorry," Pete said. "But let's be clear. You think that the others weren't just the work of some random serial killer bastard. You think that the Church took them because they fit a pattern that might have been you. Orphans. Foster children. Girls who had come suddenly to live with relatives. All matching your general physical profile and generally eternal age. Something that I missed or just didn't want to see? Do I have this now?"

Emma took a deep breath and nodded. "But not Coral," she clarified, although she could tell Pete got it. He was methodical like that. Needed to make sure he had all the pieces exactly so. She looked out at the swiftly falling snowflakes. A dozen images of Charlie Ryan filled her head, because this was all about him, too, wasn't it? Maybe she *wasn't* a bad detective. Maybe she hadn't found him because they'd gotten to him long ago—like they'd now gotten to Coral.

She turned to look at Pete. "They took her to send a message: that they know I'm here. So they have to keep her alive.

Because the only reason they'd take the wrong girl is to make the right girl surface. And that would be me."

"So, back to this Kingsley Lloyd," Pete said. Emma could see him shifting more pieces, like a huge jigsaw puzzle with no picture on the box for guidance.

"Yeah?"

"I've still got nothing on him," he said. "There're a few going by that name, but as far as I can tell, none of them are *him*. One in Wales. Another in Australia. Couple of guys in Canada. Nothing that's shouting immortal herpetologist." He smirked. "Although maybe the Aussie. Every damn picture he posts is worse than the next. He likes to wear this green porkpie hat. And Hawaiian shirts. But that wouldn't be your guy, would it?"

Despite herself, Emma laughed. "Don't think so." She pictured Kingsley Lloyd's froggy face, bowed legs, and thick, stout hands. He had worn corduroy trousers even in the Florida heat and plain cotton shirts and work boots. A handkerchief had always dangled from his back pocket. Most of all, she remembered that he always looked more tired and sweatier than anyone else down there, up until the very end. He'd always had a bone weariness that seemed to come from somewhere deep inside. She remembered him now, sipping all the lemonade in the museum gift shop. Gulping it down as though his thirst just couldn't be quenched.

Back then that had just made her uneasy. Now she wondered.

Pete's face went serious. "Em," he said, "so they might be after him, too?"

"I think so," she said, cupping her hands over her knees. "If I'm right. If he's still alive, and let's face it, I think I should have realized he *was* a long time ago." She turned to Pete, shifting in her seat. "But if I'm right and he is, there's always the other possibility, isn't there? That he's working with them."

Pete smiled fully for the first time since he'd rescued her from the fire. "Taught you well, O'Neill." The inside of the cab was growing colder, snow piling up outside, covering the windshield until he cranked the ignition and the wipers flicked it heavily away. "So now what?"

He reached to adjust the rearview mirror, waiting. Emma knew he could tell her, of course. He knew as well as she did what they needed to do. But that wasn't how it worked between her and Pete. *You talk a case out. You try not to go it alone unless you have to.*

Emma held her hands to the heater, felt her fingers warm as the hot air poured out. The smell of bacon was fainter now, but still mingling with the smell of snow and cold. Her stomach growled again. "Now," she said, "we start by finding Coral. Then the rest. But first we need to head back to my place. If someone set that fire intentionally, we need to start there. See what we can find."

"Agreed," Pete said. He shifted the truck into gear, eased over the snowy parking lot, avoiding a huge pothole near the exit toward Lemmon.

"You still owe me pancakes," she reminded him.

"If you don't get us killed first," Pete said.

"Thanks, Detective."

But she was relieved one of them had acknowledged that death was a distinct possibility.

Chapter Sixteen

England and France

1917

Charlie let the Great War in Europe swallow him whole.

He had always wanted to fly, and since the Americans were late to the party, he volunteered with the British Royal Air Force. Experience wasn't needed. His desire to fight with the Brits was enough to get him into flight school, and after that, nobody cared he was a Yank. No one had fought a war from the air before. And no one had fought a war as hugely destructive as this one.

Flying was terrifying and exhilarating and addicting in the way things are when you don't give a damn what happens to you. Just as he'd always dreamed. It came easily to him, automatic as breathing.

But it was complicated, too, more complicated than controlling a hawk. Living things made their own decisions in order to survive. Nonliving things broke down, and when that happened, more often than not, they took you down with them.

"You got to get a feel for the stick and rudder," he'd tell the rookies. "A feel for the air. It'll save your hide when the

engine conks out and you have to land in a field or worse. You glide in right and you won't break your neck."

Hawks were gliders, after all. They rarely flapped unless it was to escape.

Everyone in southern England wanted to fly with Charlie, possibly just to say they'd lived through the experience. Below them on the scarred earth of France and Germany, bodies piled up in the trenches. Later, Charlie would realize it was just the beginning, that the Treaty of Versailles didn't end the conflict as much as it simply paused things and let the Germans catch their breath, so Adolf Hitler could rise to power and make the Germans feel like they hadn't lost the first time.

That wasn't the end, either.

In point of fact, Charlie—technically forever draft-eligible as long as there was a draft—would have many future conflicts to fly right into and fight.

Charlie fought. He survived. He did not stop missing Emma any more than the grotesquely wounded soldiers missed their phantom limbs and eyes.

BACK WHEN HE *first started flying missions to France, back when somewhere below on the ground, a young Adolf Hitler was fighting against him in the Great War, he made a friend of sorts in a fellow pilot. Robert Worley was a daredevil, a prankster, a storyteller. All those Druid tales and some of the Irish myths Frank Ryan used to spin? Robert Worley knew them, too.*

Telling the old fables passed the time, helped calm the soldiers' nerves before a mission. Talking about women did that, too. Worley had a lot to say about his girlfriend Jane back in London. Jane was tall and blonde, with lips like cherries. He hailed her other parts, too, praising them with awful, bawdy odes and ballads, making the other pilots—boys, all of them, just boys—red-faced with drunken laughter.

Charlie mentioned Emma only in the abstract. The Church of Light might have already gotten to her. If they hadn't, she was living a new life. This is what he hoped for her. He was left only with memories and pain. No amount of warm beer or whiskey could quell either. So it was easier to let Worley talk.

"You know the one about Tuatha Dé Danann?" Worley grinned when Charlie told him no. "My Irish great-grandmother says they live forever, mate. But they can be killed. They've got to hide from the mortal world."

"Well," Charlie said, matter-of-factly. "That's a hell of story."

"You've got Irish in you, too, don't you? Ryan—that's Irish. So you know."

Charlie did know.

"Got another one," Worley said, the two pints he'd drunk encouraging him. He told of a town that disappeared, only to resurface after many years. Sometimes, when he let himself think about it, Charlie imagined the stream to be like that. Its magic was so powerful it couldn't just stay put . . . because everyone would know about it, would mine its possibilities. That hadn't happened.

Charlie had never believed in magic before they all drank the tea, but now he had no choice, did he?

Like many pilots, Robert had a ritual of superstitions designed to keep him safe, to ensure he made it home to England and Jane. The odds were against them even if their planes functioned perfectly; anything from a hangnail to a bad night's sleep could cause catastrophe, not to mention

*what the enemy could do. Before each mission, Robert Wor-
ley painted a Celtic cross on the side of his plane, and the
word "Danu," a fresh one of each over the last—so many
times that the cross and the word were a messy inch thick.*

"You think I'm crazy?" he asked Charlie once.

Charlie shook his head. "No crazier than I am."

*He'd tried to leave it at that. He hadn't come to Europe
and the Great War wanting friendship. Friends were something to which he no longer felt entitled. He had not been
there to save his family. He had lost Emma even if he believed
he had been protecting her. He was doomed to an endless
sameness, a seventeen-year-old body that even his reckless-
ness seemed unable to destroy.*

*On the other hand, how could he leave this world without
finding Emma again? It would be a greater sin than any he'd
already committed.*

*Still, if Charlie had allowed himself a friend, it would have
been Robert Worley.*

*Maybe that was why he'd agreed to pose together for a
single photograph with their unit during the war. He hated
the idea of nostalgia, but he understood Robert's fierce desire
to prove to Jane that he was what he'd claimed to be—a handsome soldier in a sharply pressed uniform, a hero of the skies.*

*So Charlie stood with one foot on a tree stump, his arm
draped over Worley's shoulder, both of them staring straight
and solemn into the camera—Worley's expression to act the
part, Charlie's because he felt grim.*

A FEW DAYS *later, Charlie killed a man face to face for the first
time. Worley was with him. They were shot down by the
most basic of anti-aircraft fire while on a recon mission in
the French countryside not far from Marseille.*

They'd managed to land the rickety two-seater biplane, a Royal Aircraft Factory B.E.8, as it smoked and sputtered, but just barely and with enough impact that the whole contraption split into pieces as they hit the ground.

Worley broke a leg and dislocated his collarbone, and Charlie's arm got sliced open at the meaty part near his shoulder.

They were armed, but not battle ready. Neither was ready to die. By the time he was flying over France, Charlie understood the idiocy of his choices, but the heedless anger surging through him hadn't dissipated even one tiny bit. If he had lost everything, then at least he could destroy the enemy and save the world. If he succeeded, it would be a sign. A redemption. He would find Emma someday. He would make things right again.

Robert aimed his Colt at the German soldiers who attacked them as they were still crawling from the burning wreckage of the plane they'd affectionately named Ethel, managing to get off a few stray shots. Ethel seemed a big girl's name, and the biplane was a blocky-looking old bitch that nonetheless flew like a dream unless it was hit by machine-gun fire in the fuselage.

The Germans began shooting.

It was Charlie whose aim rang true, hitting one German soldier directly in the belly, then grabbing up his bayonet as the man fell, slumping into the muddy fields that incongruously smelled of springtime along with blood and excrement and other stenches of death. A tree of some sort was blooming not far away, tiny white blossoms that, if he'd had the time, would have made Charlie's heart ache. Overhead, three black crows cawed and dipped lower in the bright blue sky. The biplane was still burning and the heat of the flames licked at Charlie's back.

Robert Worley was crawling, trying to stand.

Charlie thought of Emma, just a flash of memory. Her hair, dark and shining and wavy. Her bright eyes. The way the crook of her neck smelled damp and sweet when he nuzzled his nose against it. The taste of her when they kissed—like oranges and spice and the morning air when the ocean breeze blew cool and salty. Her softness when he pressed, hard and eager, against her. The way her body fit with his, exactly, perfectly right.

He figured he would die. Why else would his brain stop midbattle to send him these thoughts?

Instead, he charged forward, screaming sounds he had no memory of once it was all over. He plunged the bayonet into the other German, felt it stab through skin and intestines and bone. He would never forget the horrible sucking sound it made as he pulled it back out and dropped it to the earth, or the look of utter surprise on the man's face, the smell of everything that had kept him alive and ticking coming loose and undone. The way he choked and gagged. The bright red of his blood. How his knees crumpled as he fell, with an odd grace, just as a white, billowy cloud drifted lazily above them.

"Ach," the man said. Only that. He fell forward, his face hitting Charlie's boots. He quivered a few times, and was still.

Charlie had to push him away, then turned him face up and knelt at his side. With his thumbs, he closed the man's eyes. A crow cawed.

"Jesus Christ," Robert Worley was saying over and over. Charlie turned.

Robert Worley was clutching his chest, a dark blood seeping out between his fingers, spatters of red drops dotting his nose and cheeks like freckles.

A few drops had splashed his chin, too, staining already

grimy skin—a face that was marred by bumps of acne. Robert Worley loved his Jane, but he was just a boy. He was no hero of the skies, no matter how hard he pretended.

Charlie stumbled across the battle-pocked earth and knelt beside his friend. Robert Worley held out his hand. Charlie took it until it was over.

"Tell Jane," Worley said, his voice fading as his eyes stayed on Charlie's.

"I will," Charlie said, trying not to cry. Robert Worley was just twenty years old. Charlie Ryan would always and forever be seventeen. In that moment, he felt one hundred. The dead Germans' papers identified them as Jochen Liebold, age eighteen, from Düsseldorf; and Gerhardt Arnd, nineteen, from Mannheim.

When no one came for any of them, neither the Brits nor the Germans, Charlie dug their graves. He marked the turned ground with stones, and on Robert's he etched his copilot's name onto the top stone. Somehow he worked his way back to safe French territory alone. It took him over a week of sleepless scavenging—long enough that the RAF assumed that he and Worley were both dead. Quite the happy kerfuffle when he turned up alive, filthy and starving, and quite another shift in emotion when his commanders realized Worley wasn't with him.

AFTER THAT CHARLIE went through the motions. Told his superiors he was ready to fly another mission as soon as a plane was available to replace Ethel. Found a way to send a telegram to Jane MacMillan in Leeds.

Charlie would always believe that Robert Worley's death was in some way his fault. He had been reckless. He had been lost and self-destructive and courting the one thing it *was most difficult for him to find: death. There was only one thing for him now. He would find his way home. He would destroy those who wanted him gone. And he would find Emma O'Neill and tell her he had lied. Or he would die trying.*

Chapter Seventeen

There was a trail. There was a pattern. There had to be. That's how people worked. They left trails; they lived according to patterns—even when they were desperate to hide both. Emma O'Neill and Detective Pete Mondragon, sitting hip to hip at Emma's kitchen table, needed those patterns to appear. Soon. It might already be too late.

"This is the neighborhood where Elodie's body was found," Emma said, pointing to the map of Dallas displays on her laptop. "And this is the church where she was last seen." She pointed to a spot to the west. "Which is approximately two miles from where she lived."

Pete leaned toward the screen, elbows knocking against the detritus of the burger takeout they'd picked up, which was probably more suited for detective work than pancakes, anyway. It wasn't pancakes, but Pete had promised to feed her, and Pete Mondragon never went back on a promise.

Once he had told her that her eating habits were like those of a thirteen-year-old boy. She didn't disagree. It was something they had in common.

Most of the tenants on Emma's floor had found other accommodations, per management's request. But returning wasn't forbidden, and Emma was a stubborn girl when it came to things that scared her. Even smoke and fire. Particularly a fire that might have been set to burn her alive. She and Pete had scouted the building as best they could, but a clear cause for the fire had yet to present itself. The snow had stopped, and the arson investigators were gone for the night.

No answers on that front meant they needed to focus on where the hell Coral might be.

Emma jabbed a finger at the screen again. "Look, here's where we are, right near where Coral lives." She gestured briefly at the window over her kitchen sink, the one that looked out on the street. "Just a few houses from here."

Then she scrolled the map to the west and then north. "Here's her high school." More scrolling. "And here's Hugo's house. And the club they go to sometimes in Deep Ellum. And this one, off Hall. I, um, was with them there just the other night."

No need to mention the whole Matt debacle. No need to add her other personal failings to the long list of things that weren't going right. Pete pushed up the nosepiece of his thick black glasses. She'd helped him pick out the frames online, insisting that they looked good even though he'd balked at anything trendier than his decade-old pair with scratches on the lenses.

At the time, bristling at his fussiness, she'd thought of her sister Lucy. She'd hated wearing her spectacles even though her eyesight was weak for close work like reading or knitting. "I like a girl in spectacles," Charlie had told Lucy after she'd gotten her first pair, with a sly wink at Emma. She could still picture the way her sister had blushed, her sulky mood melting away . . .

Emma shoved the memory aside. Pete peered at the laptop screen. "So no one has reported seeing Coral since the morning she disappeared, correct?" he asked. "And it was vacation, so she wouldn't have gone to school. Her parents say she was asleep when they left, and gone when they returned. No sign of a struggle. And her boyfriend didn't hear from her, either. Not a phone call or a text. And he even gave his phone to that cop that night, correct?"

"So he said." Emma absently crunched a Cheeto, less out of hunger than anxiety. She pondered Hugo. She trusted him more than she trusted most people. But her hunches had been wrong before. Did he really not know where Coral was headed that day? If there had been cell phones back in St. Augustine, she would have wanted to communicate with Charlie every second.

No; she'd spent time with Hugo in the immediate aftermath. If that panic was a flawless act, well, then he was a lot more dangerous than anyone had guessed. Another possibility: he knew where Coral was headed; he just didn't want *Emma* to know. Emma may have trusted him, but maybe the feeling wasn't mutual.

Anything was possible when people had secrets. And *everyone* had secrets. Even people you trusted. Maybe even especially the people you trusted, because they had an investment in maintaining that trust.

"No dead bodies matching her description have turned up," Pete said. "So we've got that in our favor."

Emma didn't want to think about that. She *couldn't* think about that. Coral was alive. Somewhere. They'd find her, and they'd get her to a hospital.

"Oh," she said. "I—oh." How had she not realized?

"You got something, O'Neill?" Pete's gaze was sharp.

Yes. It was possible.

"Maybe," she said. "If Coral is bait for me, then they wouldn't have gone far, would they? That wouldn't make sense. But that's not the only thing. Not the *important* thing. Because they made Elodie sick, remember? They poisoned her, just like they poisoned Allie Golden. To see if she could *get* sick. Which means they had to have taken her to a place to experiment on her. I've been focusing on the idea that they'd held Elodie at a house or an apartment. But looking at this map, I've been thinking about the cover story I gave Coral and Hugo. That I was studying to be a nurse. I didn't pick that out of a hat; half the people who live around here are involved in the medical profession." She jabbed at the screen with an orange-dusted finger. "It's the—"

"Medical center," Pete said, and he patted her on the back.

Emma drew closer to the map, squinting at hospital after hospital. Methodist. Parkland. Children's. Baylor. Dozens of walk-in clinics of various sizes.

Pete rubbed his thumb over his narrow chin. The crow's-feet at his eyes deepened as he frowned again at the screen. "So you think Elodie and Coral were taken by someone with access to poisons or disease cultures? You're right; there's lots of research here in Dallas. Especially after that Ebola scare a couple years back."

Emma dug for another Cheeto, then decided against it. "Yeah, that explains Elodie. But not Coral. I mean, if they *do* know Coral's not me, then why make her sick? Isn't that a waste of resources? Or maybe they want me to think they've made a mistake. Picked a girl who doesn't fit the whole profile. So I'll think they're slipping up. And they think they're leading me to her so they can grab me and . . . I don't know."

It still didn't make sense. And even the parts that sort of

did couldn't help them; nothing pinpointed where Coral had been taken, or even *if* she had been taken. Not for sure. On a hunch, Emma reached for her phone. She punched in Hugo's number, not even sure what she was going to say.

He answered on the first ring.

"What aren't you telling me?" she asked without saying hello.

There was a long silence. She couldn't even hear him breathe. For a moment she wondered if the connection had broken.

When he finally answered, his voice cracked.

"I wasn't completely honest with you."

"Oh?"

"We did fight, me and Coral. It wasn't anything much. Just silly crap about how she thought maybe I didn't want to get an apartment with her next year. That once we were in college, I'd want to find someone else. Get tired of her, I guess. You know how some guys do. But I would never! That's bullshit. And she said—she said she was gonna ask you. That you never said, but she knew you understood about love. That she could tell there was a history that you . . . That's all pretty lame, I know."

"Not lame," Emma said evenly. "Honest."

Hugo took a deep breath on the other end. "She said she was gonna ask you. And you know Coral. She does what she says she's going to. So I guess what I'm saying is, I know you hadn't seen her, but maybe she was trying to find you when she disappeared. You think that's possible?"

She could have told him that he was an idiot for keeping this quiet. That Coral could be dead, or worse than dead. So why, why couldn't he have just told the truth? Both to her, and to that nosy cop with the ponytail? But there was no point in calling the proverbial kettle black. Emma had told Coral and Hugo some half-baked story about spending the holidays with a study group. Had her own lies about going to Brookhaven somehow made Coral an easier target, or just a target to begin with? *The* target?

"Maybe," she said finally. "I'll call you when I know more. Hang in there, Hugo. It's going to be okay."

Pete reached over and powered down Emma's laptop. "Where to?" he asked.

"Brookhaven Community College," Emma said. "I think she went there to find me. There's a nursing program there. I told Coral I was a student. That I was in this study group over the holidays. Shit. Maybe someone saw something." She scooped up her bag and headed to the door. "C'mon."

He stayed seated. "It's almost midnight, O'Neill."

Emma's shoulders sagged. "Oh," she said, and the adrenaline coursing through her veins melted away. Now in addition to being terrified for Coral, she felt exhausted and faintly embarrassed.

Pete rose and walked to her couch. "You got an extra blanket?" he asked. "Unless you're not comfortable with me bunking here. I didn't have time to get a room yet, but I can—"

"It's fine," she said. "It's all gonna smell like smoke."

"I've been in worse," Pete said.

"Me, too."

LATER, LYING ON her bed, Emma stared at the pocket watch she'd hung up. She didn't even bother to pull back the comforter. She wasn't about to sleep. Not tonight. Why did she hold on to this heavy, ridiculous thing, anyway? To prove she had been loved once. That there had been a boy who had given her his heart.

In the dim light filtering through the window from outside, she studied the outlines of the flying hawk etched on the case. She remembered the way the metal felt cool against her skin when she wore it. How happy it made Charlie to give her this beautiful gift. How shallow and silly she'd been even to mention its weight.

Emma sat up and took the watch into her hand. She traced the shape of the hawk with her finger. Charlie had lied to her that day on the road, or rather, he had not told her the full truth. Hawks wanted their freedom, yes. They were temperamental, and sometimes you had to wait them out. But those goshawks that Charlie had so carefully tended—they mated for life. They found the one for them and they didn't let go.

She would keep on searching, not just for Coral, but for Charlie. She wouldn't give up. Because she didn't want the watch to be the only good thing she had left.

Chapter Eighteen

Florida and beyond

1918

Charlie headed back to America after the Armistice with no home, no job, no family, and no Emma. He had left the one person he never should have, and now she could be anywhere. And why? Because at seventeen you do very stupid things, believing with all your heart that they are not stupid at all.

His goals were the same as they had been since Worley's death. Find Emma O'Neill and tell her what an ass he'd been. And destroy Glen Walters—if he still lived—and burn his Church of Light to the ground.

He wondered briefly about Kingsley Lloyd. Charlie suspected that the bastard had also drunk the tea. But that wasn't his problem. The world was a big place, and no doubt Kingsley Lloyd had run as far away from the O'Neills and Ryans as he could. Maybe he'd dried up the stream and taken the plants. Anything was possible.

So when his ship docked in New York, Charlie hopped a train to Florida. Cautiously, he investigated. Asked people when it seemed safe. Even asked after the Fountain of Youth, hoping Emma was trying to find it, too. She'd seemed so *desperate for the water and its plants that last day. If he was already down in the Everglades—in the midst of the Juan Ponce de León legends, none of which had subsided, not even the tiniest bit—then he might as well ask about the fountain. Maybe there would be something that would lead him to Emma.*

He hunted through St. Augustine late one evening, sneaking through the darkness, his heart pounding, the sadness filling him in a visceral way that took him by surprise. He had thought that the war had numbed his ability to feel. It had not.

The burned shell of the Alligator Farm and Museum was gone. A civic center had replaced it. The sign out front advertised an orchestral concert the coming evening. All that was left of what had once been a vibrant business was the path that led behind the building to a small, deep pool—once the gator observation pool, where the tourists could watch them swim and feed. Now it was filled with koi and other small fish. The huge aviary had been torn down and replaced with grass, benches, and a white gazebo.

Other families occupied the house he'd lived in and Emma's house, too. It was as though the O'Neills and Ryans had never existed.

The ache inside nearly overwhelmed him, but he forced himself to explore and make sure there was nothing here that he needed to know about.

There was indeed nothing. That hurt just as much.

Glen Walters had taken his traveling show of hate to places unknown. If any of his followers remained around St. Augustine, they were keeping quiet about it. The fire had burned out in more ways than one.

After that the tiny town of Punta Gorda. A natural spring

near St. Petersburg. And half a dozen hamlets and towns in between. Nothing. If he was looking for proof of the magical waters, he would find them in the mirror and nowhere else— a daily truth that made him want to both laugh and weep.

And so he continued, up and down and across the country, then up to parts of Canada and south to Mexico and eventually even back to Europe, on a hunch that Emma might have gone looking for the Ryan relatives who had supposedly passed down all those tales of immortality that Charlie's father had loved to tell. He listened and looked and remained patient like his falconry training had taught him. He would find her. The human network of stories and gossip and the random but continual interconnections of one place to another, of someone who knew someone who might know something, fueled his search.

This would not end like Robert Worley's story, a man lying dead in a foreign field. He wouldn't let it.

CHARLIE DISCOVERED A *talent for vagrancy. He took jobs as he needed, never growing too attached to anyone or anything, always staying long enough just to make what money he could and then moving on. Always quiet, always polite, never attracting attention. He changed his name as it suited him. Bland names. He was Benjamin Hollis while he lived in Chicago. Charlie Murray in Boston. Briefly, he boxed under that name. He was broke and they were paying.*

"You're one hell of a brawler," the trainer told him. "Where'd you learn to fight like that?"

"In the war," Charlie said, which was true.

He moved on the day he saw they'd put his picture on a poster. Notoriety was good only if he controlled it.

He worked at zoos. He tended aviaries and private

menageries and veterinary hospitals. No one had steadier hands with frightened animals than Charlie Ryan.

One day at a vet practice in Louisville, a girl brought in a mangy mutt, back leg gone lame. Doc Barrow was out at a horse farm, tending to a difficult birth.

"Let me see," Charlie told the girl. "You stand by his face and talk soft to him so he's not scared."

He ran his fingers slowly and thoughtfully over the dog's leg and hip, his eyes closed as he concentrated. Doc Barrow was a good teacher and Charlie loved to learn. He would hate for the pup to be lame so young. Then he felt it: A muscle in the leg. Not torn, he didn't think. No. Not grave after all.

"Your pup has a sprained muscle," he told the girl. "You need to keep him quiet for a few days. No running around. I think it should heal on its own just fine."

He was right.

Barrow offered to make his job permanent. He needed a reliable apprentice.

"I'll be moving on," Charlie told him. "But thanks."

Another possible life that he had no choice but to leave.

IN A DARK *moment, he considered becoming a daredevil pilot and crashing in a ball of fire, a fleeting moment of fame, a way to proclaim, Charlie Ryan was here! Everyone else in the flying business wanted notoriety these days: barnstormers and wing walkers and flagpole sitters.*

Instead, he found a series of jobs flying crop dusters. The Agricultural Department of the US government was developing a domestic purpose for airplanes.

"You're gonna make a ton of cash," the guy who'd first hired him promised, a guy now long dead and gone.

The guy had been right, of course. Lots of other people

hired him after that; he couldn't stay longer than a year dusting the same farmland for obvious reasons. Every gig was two years, tops. But America was big and wide. It was mostly farms.

Charlie kept to himself the notion that if he continued flying, if he stayed aloft and moving, he might even spot Emma someday from the sky—spot her far below in some random place. Stranger things had happened.

The fact that he was still living and still seventeen was proof of that.

So he flew, every plane he could get his hands on. A Fokker like those ones the Germans had flown in the Great War. A Moth, so easy to handle that he would forget his grief for a while as he looped and soared.

One day, as he headed back to the room he was renting in a boarding house just outside of Monterey, California, he bought a paper from the newsboy on the corner. Charlie had made it a habit to scour the various periodicals. Nothing had ever appeared, but you never knew. Something could lead him to Emma.

That something occurred one night in the early fall of 1925, in the form of a story on page seven.

Charlie stared at the page, his eyes scanning. His breath seized momentarily in his lungs. A traveling preacher named Glen Walters had died of a sudden and massive stroke after a series of tent revivals in Alabama.

According to the story, one of his followers, a man named Norman Thigpen, had taken over the preaching the next night.

This by itself might not have made the papers. But Thigpen's talk of the need to root out evil had inspired the brief resurgence of a chapter of the Ku Klux Klan, who, in a brutal *display of their brand of American justice, kidnapped a girl with long dark hair, beat her, then cut off her hair and chained her to a telephone pole. The story was that she'd been accused of immoral behavior, the specifics of that left vague. What happened after that was unclear. Rumors abounded that it wasn't even the Klan, but some other group with its own shadowy agenda.*

When the initial shock wore off, Charlie understood the girl was not Emma. But the story stuck with him nonetheless, and not just because that bastard Glen Walters was dead. Or because there was a trail to follow, even though he sensed it wouldn't lead him to Emma.

Something was happening. He just wasn't sure what it was.

What he was sure of though, was this: The Church of Light was evolving. It was hiding in plain sight, ever on the move as he was. And wherever Emma was, she was like that, too. All of them, like that ever-disappearing town in Robert Worley's story.

And he also knew this, although he wasn't quite sure what to do about it: killing Walters wouldn't bring back what he'd lost. If the war had taught Charlie one lesson, it was that killing accomplished only death.

Chapter Nineteen

Just before six thirty the next morning, Emma and Pete parked at the edge of the Brookhaven campus. The sun had yet to rise; it was still dark, not even a hint of dawn. The snow had stopped, but a stronger cold front had blown through, and the temperature hovered just above freezing.

Emma pulled her black peacoat tight around her as she climbed out of Pete's truck. Her hair whipped wildly in the wind, and she dug into her pocket for an elastic, then swiped it back into a messy tail. On this broad, open campus with its anonymous-looking cement buildings, Dallas felt suddenly like a windy prairie.

Pete followed silently, chugging coffee from a large Styrofoam cup, his expression both alert and weary in that distinctive cop way he had, dark eyes scanning and missing nothing. He hadn't shaved, but he wore a fresh gray Henley shirt under his jacket, and the same jeans and boots as yesterday.

He traveled light. It was a habit Emma understood quite well.

Their plan wasn't much to speak of. Mostly they were here to nose around while the students began slowly filling the campus. Catch people early enough before they were sufficiently caffeinated, and maybe they'd be more open. Emma had no idea if this plan would work, no idea if it was any more than a wild-goose chase. She had finally slept, but fitfully, snatches of dreamless oblivion punctuated by wide-awake brain churning.

Across the parking lot, a few windows in the main building of the campus were already lit. Classes began early. Emma appreciated the practicality of this. If she ever went to college, maybe she'd start here.

"Nursing school building's over there," she said. She'd looked it up when she'd told Coral and Hugo that series of lies—always best to make them as believable as possible, with a solid foundation of knowledge and fact.

As the sun rose, the campus slowly rose to life with it.

OVER THE NEXT two hours. Emma and Pete talked to everyone they spotted. A tall girl in scrubs and a Navajo-print hooded jacket. Two guys drinking Starbucks. A middle-aged woman who turned out to be the head of the nurse practitioner program. A tired-looking man with a goatee who was actually looking for the computer science building but had gotten lost.

"Have you seen this girl?" Emma asked each one of them. She held up the picture of Coral on her phone.

No. No. No.

At just past nine o'clock, two girls who looked to be in their twenties exited from the side of the nursing building. Emma strode toward them, Pete following at a distance. This was their system.

"We're looking for a missing girl," she called, waggling

her phone at them. She let the word *missing* sink in. Then she moved closer.

One had a streak of pink in her blonde hair and eyebrows plucked so thin they resembled two commas on her forehead. The other was wearing a Rangers ball cap, her long brown ponytail threaded through the back.

"Don't know her," said the one with pink streak, squinting at Coral's picture.

The one with ball cap looked up from the image. "That's the girl whose parents went on TV, right?" Her face went pale, and her gaze shifted from Emma to Pete, who was now standing beside her. "Y'all cops or something?"

"Private investigators," Emma said. "This is my partner, Detective Mondragon." Emma slid her PI license from her pocket. Of course, Texas did not have reciprocity with the state next door, so the document was invalid. Not that these two would have any idea. Anyway, she didn't have time to apply for a new set of papers every time she jumped to a new place. It was highly inconvenient. As was everything she had to do to keep her actual fingerprints out of any government data bank.

"Have you seen her?" Pete asked the girls, his voice pleasant, almost conversational. Pete managed to make even an interrogation sound like he was just shooting the breeze.

Ball Cap hesitated. "You know, maybe I did see her," she said. "Afternoon of New Year's Eve."

Emma waited, just as Pete had taught her. She sensed the girl would fill in the blanks, but only if she wasn't pushed. The silence stretched on.

"You notice anything particular?" Pete asked finally, in that same genial *Hey, y'all, let's go get a drink* voice.

Ball Cap ran her tongue across the inside of her bottom

lip. Shifted her gaze to her friend and then back to Emma and Pete. "She was at the student center. I stopped to get a coffee before going home. Place was pretty empty, closing early. They wouldn't even make me a latte, just that crap regular stuff. Anyway, I'm pretty sure I saw her over at the bookstore across from the food court. They'd locked up already, but she was talking to some guy."

"You sure it was *this* girl?" Emma asked. She held up Coral's picture again. Hugo had sent her the photo when it first became clear something bad had happened. It was actually of both Coral and Emma, but Emma had cropped herself out.

"And the guy?" Pete's tone toughened just a little, and she sensed him rise just so slightly on his feet, like a runner waiting for the starting gunshot. "Was he old? Young? Somewhere in between? Had you ever seen him before?"

The girl paused. The hairs on the nape of Emma's neck stood up, although if Pete had asked her why, she couldn't have said. Just that she had felt this in other moments, in other years, in other places. An overwhelming sense that everything was about to change.

"Nothing special," the girl said. "The guy, I mean. He was medium height." She held her hand a few inches above her head. "Blond. He needed a shave. Cute, though. He was, I don't know, thirty, maybe? Maybe younger. She seemed to know him. I'm pretty positive about that. That's about all I remember. I—oh! He was wearing this preppy polo shirt—*so* not my thing, but like I said, he was cute—and he had this tattoo on his arm, which made up for it, you know? It said, BELIEVE."

Emma froze. Her lungs momentarily seized up. "What?" she coughed.

She felt more than saw Pete's sharp glare.

The girl frowned. The nausea rose without warning, pooling in Emma's throat. She absolutely, positively couldn't have been *that* stupid . . .

"The tattoo," she managed. "Describe it again."

After a dramatic eye roll, the girl sighed. Then she spoke slowly and deliberately, indicating that Emma was either an idiot or acting like one—she would have been happy to know Emma herself agreed that this was absolutely, positively the case. "The. Word. BELIEVE. On. His. Forearm. In. Blue. Can I go now?"

"Shit," Emma said. "Shit. Shit. Shit."

"She means in a minute," Pete muttered. He put a hand on her arm, but Emma shook it off. She was very worried she would vomit. Matt, whose last name she did not know. Matt, who quoted war movies. Matt, who was drunkenly fascinated by how young she looked. Matt, who flirted with Coral and then turned to Emma. Matt, who came home with her. To her apartment. Where she lived. Matt who had run his fingers over the pocket watch that Charlie had given her. Matt who had been there in the morning.

Who the hell was he, really? The new face of the Church of Light? Whoever he was, he had known all along who *she* was. There was no other explanation. She was sad and lonely and stupid. And he had tracked her to the bar while she thought she was tracking Elodie's killer. While she was keeping an eye on Coral, although obviously she'd failed miserably there. He'd watched. And waited. And now . . .

She had seen the tattoo and not given it a second thought. Had never bothered for one second to possibly connect it to whoever was trying to flush her out. To the Church of Light. The people who thought she was the embodiment of evil. The people who wanted her dead. Even though Glen Walters had shouted that exact word from his pulpit probably a thousand times in the swamps of Florida, over a hundred years ago.

Matt had known who she was. And she had invited him home with her.

Shit. Shit. Shit.

He had slept in her damn bed. And now Coral was missing. Without thinking, Emma placed her hands on Ball Cap's shoulders.

"Em," Pete warned.

The girl tried to shake free. "Hey, lemme go!"

Her friend with the pink streak shoved Emma's arm. But Emma tightened her grip. "Did you hear anything else? Anything. Think hard. Did Coral say anything to him? You have to remember something else. It was just you and your damn coffee. Think."

The world was slipping and sliding, the years were jamming together, and all Emma could think was that she had lived *so many years*—but she would always be the same as she was that day in 1913 when Kingsley Lloyd insisted they all drink that horrid tea. Always and forever a silly seventeen-year-old girl. Wily but impatient. Wanting what she wanted when she wanted it: Answers. Certainty. Charlie Ryan.

"I'm gonna call the cops," Pink Streak said, fishing for her phone.

"We *are* the cops," Pete muttered, but his eyes were on Emma. "Let her go, Miss O'Neill. Just walk away. Whatever this is, just walk away."

Emma blinked hard a few times. The years faded, as they always did, stranding her in the present. So she did what he asked. She let go.

The girls ran, uttering a rich assortment of vulgarities that would have shocked even the likes of Frank Ryan. Had Emma been less distracted, she would have been impressed with the variety. But her gaze landed on Matt—he of the BELIEVE tattoo—stepping around the corner of the nursing building. Her pulse exploded.

"Pete," she began, but something hard and blunt smacked the back of her head.

Her vision went dim even as she heard Pete yell her name. Then there was the sound of a fist hitting a face. She tried to run, or imagined she did, and her brain sent her images of Coral along with a terrible fear that it had all gone so very wrong.

Someone pressed a cloth to her mouth, and she smelled something vile and thick, and after a moment there was only blackness.

SHE WOKE UP some time later—she wasn't sure how long, but it couldn't have been that long—bound to a chair in what seemed to be an abandoned warehouse. So much for her medical school facility theory. Although, maybe this had once been a warehouse for medical supplies.

Pete was slumped in a chair across the room. Emma's head ached from the blow to the back of her skull, but whatever chemical they'd used to knock her out was no doubt coursing harmlessly through her veins or had already evaporated.

Matt was nowhere to be seen.

But her head was actually throbbing pretty hard, now that she realized it. She vomited neatly—as neatly as she could while lashed in place—on the filthy cement floor. Almost right away she felt better. Then she looked around. It was damp and cold. It smelled like mold and ammonia and dead things.

"I thought they'd killed you," a girl's voice rasped from behind her.

Coral! Emma wrenched her neck trying to catch a glimpse

over her shoulder. *Yes. Coral. Alive!* Tied to a cot, but Coral was alive. Tears stung Emma's eyes.

"You're here," she managed. She sniffed and tried to wriggle in her chair, tried to look more directly at Coral, but her neck was stiff and not turning properly, and her vision was doing something wonky that made her want to vomit again. She couldn't move her hands. Her fingers felt swollen, numb.

"Oh, my God, Emma," Coral croaked. Her voice sounded thin and papery, as if her throat were parched. "How did you find me? Where's Hugo? Oh my God. They—"

"It's going to be okay," Emma interrupted. She immediately regretted saying that. No use lying anymore. She'd told enough lies, enough to land Coral here. With a violent twist, she spun a few inches in the hard-backed chair. *There.* Emma swallowed. Coral was filthy, had lost weight; her cheeks were red and her forehead damp with sweat under stringy, lank hair. Dark circles ringed her hollow eyes. The red and blue streaks had faded into the brown. Her breathing seemed labored, and there was a heavy, wet rattle as she lapsed into a hacking cough.

Something clicked in Emma's bruised and disoriented brain. *They made Coral sick. They didn't have to, but they did, anyway.* This was bad. Very bad.

"I thought they were gonna kill you," Coral said again.

"I'm not that easy to kill," Emma answered. She hoped she sounded feistier than she felt. She struggled to muster a brave smile for Coral's sake.

A few feet away, Pete moaned.

Emma kept the smile frozen on her face. She'd told Coral the truth. She was not that easy to kill. But she definitely could be killed. And the people who'd tied her to this chair wanted her dead—along with Pete and Coral, of course. More collateral damage in a hundred-year hunt.

Chapter Twenty

Alabama had turned out to be a dead end. Norman Thigpen and anything connected to the Church of Light had absolutely dropped out of sight.

As for Charlie, all he had ever wanted was to keep Emma safe.

By 1939 he'd come to care less about his own safety. Over two decades had passed since he'd held Emma in his arms. Planes had gotten better, but that wasn't much comfort. Pilots had, too. Charles Lindbergh had flown solo across the Atlantic. Lucky Lindy they called him. On the other hand, a woman pilot named Amelia Earhart and her sole crewmember, Fred Noonan, had disappeared over the Pacific two years ago. She had moxie, that Amelia. Charlie seen her now and then over the years, although only peripherally. She was, he realized, a year younger than he was. Or at least she would have been. She was forty when she went missing, probably dead at the bottom of the ocean. Charlie should have been forty-one.

Life remained a strange crapshoot for most people—for everyone but Charlie Ryan, anyway.

War had broken out again in Europe. Charlie wanted to go back there, to fly and to fight. It would take a little artifice, but twenty years gone meant he could pass himself off as Charlie Ryan, Jr. Any uncanny resemblance would just be a strong familial likeness. So he'd quit his crop-dusting gig and hitched back to New York City.

He lingered for a while, settling up the arrangements. The extra few days changed everything.

One gray afternoon in October with sleet to match his mood, Charlie was hurrying down Seventh Avenue to catch the subway at Seventy-Second. He wasn't sure what made him look across the street, but when he did, he skidded to a stop, nearly falling on the slick sidewalk. There, in the window of the drugstore across the wide boulevard, was a familiar figure. One with an unmistakable frog-like face.

Kingsley Lloyd sat at the lunch counter eating a sandwich.

Charlie's heart shook wildly, like the propeller on his doomed biplane, Ethel. *He hadn't seen Kingsley Lloyd since the herpetologist had disappeared from St. Augustine.*

It can't be, *he thought.*

But it was. And like Charlie, the man hadn't aged a day.

Charlie crossed the street, weaving between the automobiles rushing in both directions, barely avoiding an oncoming car. He walked into the store so swiftly that out in the street, the driver who almost hit him was still laying on the horn.

"You're alive," Charlie barked. Of course, he'd suspected as much for a while, but seeing it in the flesh was another matter entirely. His brain struggled to process it. He remembered that time in 1916 in North Carolina. Had that been Kingsley Lloyd, too, that brief glimpse of someone who looked familiar?

Lloyd's wide face went slack. His jaw dropped. He looked as though he was seeing a ghost. "I thought you were dead."

Charlie assessed this. "No, you didn't," he said. Then he socked Kingsley Lloyd square in the jaw—a haymaker that sent the little man sprawling to the dirty floor of the five-and-dime. "That's for letting us drink that stuff."

A collective gasp rose from the other patrons; the next thing Charlie knew, the cook was grabbing his arms and trying to pin them back. A man in a wool overcoat tried to lift Kingsley Lloyd off the floor, but Lloyd seemed to be resisting, possibly so Charlie—who easily wrestled free of the cook— couldn't hit him again.

Two blue-uniformed cops shouldered their way into the five-and-dime. The shorter cop grabbed Charlie and, with a violent wrench, succeeded in pinning his arms in a way the cook couldn't.

"Everything's jake," Charlie gasped between clenched teeth. "My, um, uncle here's a little hot-headed sometimes. Aren't you, Unc?"

There was more commotion then, and a bit of tricky negotiation with the cops.

"Just fine, my little nephew," Lloyd grunted.

OUTSIDE THE SLEET *morphed briefly into rain. As if by mutual plan, Charlie and Kingsley Lloyd walked east together, pounding the wet pavement, putting distance between themselves and the cops.*

"You knew," Charlie said finally, "when you gave our fathers that plant and told them to brew it. You knew what it would do."

Charlie's strides were long; Lloyd scuttled to keep up. "I

*didn't. I swear. Now the polio prevention, that was some-
thing—"*

*"Shut up!" Charlie turned abruptly, almost knocking into
the little man, grabbing his shoulders hard with both hands.
"Don't lie to me." He studied Lloyd's face. Even in a rage,
Charlie knew how to be still. The man's cheeks were mottled
and blotchy. Was he sick? But Lloyd still looked exactly as he
had in 1916, which meant he was immortal, just like Charlie and Emma. Had he always been unwell? Charlie tried to
remember. He thought Lloyd had looked better right before
he disappeared, but what did it even matter?*

*The rain and mist had flattened Kingsley Lloyd's hair.
Honestly, sick or not, he looked even more amphibian-like
than before. "I . . . I wasn't sure," he said at last.*

*Charlie dug his fingers harder into Lloyd's shoulders,
thumbs shifting to the man's clavicle and then higher to his
carotid arteries. He could feel Kingsley Lloyd's pulse jolt
beneath his hands. "So you gambled with our lives. My parents'. Our brothers' and sisters'. Mine and Emma's. Do you
know what you took from us? For what? And now she's
gone, and—"*

*"It's not what you think," Lloyd protested. "God, it's
really not. I mean look at yourself. You're exactly the same as
you were. It's a miracle, you know. A damn miracle. You are
the same, right? You haven't noticed any changes, have you?"*

*In the Great War, Charlie had lost track of how many
dead bodies he had seen. But what had never left him—would
never leave him—was the utter strangeness of what it felt like
to take another man's life. Or the terrible sadness of watching
a friend's life slip away, with no power to save him.*

*"Have you ever figured out how many ways we actually
can be killed?" Charlie asked calmly. Lloyd's pulse rocketed*

again under his fingers. "Fire, obviously. Drowning, I'd assume, but who knows? Poison's a no-go, clearly. But if I shot you in the head, would that do it? Threw you in front of a subway train?"

"Jesus Christ, man," Lloyd whispered. "Let go of me. I didn't know they'd come after you like that. Glen Walters and his people."

Charlie tightened his grip. Either Kingsley Lloyd was also hiding from Glen Walters and his Church of Light, or he was in league with them. Charlie suspected it was the former. But he had to be certain.

Lloyd's bug eyes protruded. "Your father was smarter than he knew. Than any of you knew. Those stories he told about your ancestors—"

"Shut up," Charlie said, but his heart gave a twinge. "I don't want to talk about my family. I sure as hell don't want you to."

"I'm trying to explain."

"You're trying to save your skin." But Charlie eased his grip, and after a few seconds, he let the man go.

"Listen, Charlie." Lloyd swallowed audibly, his sharp Adam's apple bobbing. A vein had burst in his cheek during the attempted choking, leaving a thin red line just at the fleshy spot below his left eye. "Your father was right. But you've known that since Florida. There is a Fountain of Youth. It was the stream on that island."

"And the part I don't know?"

Lloyd cleared his throat noisily. "It didn't stay there. That's how it works. It disappears and pops up somewhere else, as far as I can tell. I believe there's more than one, actually, although I haven't yet figured that part out—"

"That drink of yours was a one-shot deal, Mr. Lloyd. We

don't need the damn fountain. What I want to know is why you left. Left all of us to—" Charlie reached for Lloyd again and the other man back-pedaled swiftly, almost stumbling. *If the situation hadn't been life or death, it might have been comical.*

"I knew they were on to us," Lloyd's words came in a nervous rush. *"Walters and his Church of Light believers. So I left. I went back to the island first, and it was all . . . I never should have talked to them when . . . I never imagined that they'd . . . You have to understand. I didn't believe any of us would actually find a real way to eternal life. I just imagined there were things in the earth that we could use to prolong living. To keep us young. Cheat nature a little at her own game."*

Charlie's shoulders sagged. The rain had slowed to a drizzle.

"You know we found the stream that day we went looking for iguanas. Your father and Art and I—you know none of us had ever seen it before. But it was like what I'd read. All those stories of aloe vera plants that healed or jellyfish and lobsters that lived years and years and years. I just had to know what to do." Here Lloyd paused dramatically. *"It felt like destiny."*

"With all due respect, Mr. Lloyd, screw destiny," Charlie said.

Lloyd gave a small, tight smile. *"This plant on the edge of the stream—it looked a lot like one that grew in the forests along the Amazon. The people would brew the crushed powder into a drink and swore it kept them from illness. So I thought, why not? It couldn't hurt. I knew it wasn't poisonous. But if I told all of you that my grandmother was a healer, that she knew about these things, then it would sound* legitimate, you know? And if it worked, well, not only would you all be protected from polio, but then I . . ." He paused. "I could get your father and Emma's to take me on as a partner."

"Christ." The weight of everything that had happened since then squeezed Charlie's heart. So many lives forever altered or lost—his entire immediate family gone!—because of the possibility of a business deal?

"At the time," Lloyd said, "it seemed a grand idea." And then more quietly, he added, "If I could've, I'd have run off with the lot of it." He sighed. "I'm a selfish man. Self-preservation and all that. If I'd known I'd found a miracle, you think I'd have shared it with all of you just like that?"

Charlie sneered. "But it was okay to try it on us first. That didn't bother you?"

Lloyd shrugged. "I drank the damn stuff, too. The next day, actually. Again, I thought, why not?" He was silent then, for a long time. The wind whipped around them.

Eventually he said, "Glen Walters overheard me talking to Art O'Neill. It was about a year after we all, well, you know. We were at the museum. By the gator pool. Art was worried about Emma's baby brother. About him looking so young still even though he was turning three. And it hit me then—something in the way he said it—that I hadn't brewed a cure to polio. I'd brewed a cure to everything. It was a great shock. You may not believe me, but it was. I said as much to Art, but I don't think he believed me. Not yet. But then I looked up after Art walked off, and there were Glen Walters and that little wife of his, standing by the seats where people watched the show, just staring at me, their mouths hanging open."

So that had been that. The rest Charlie knew. The slow, insidious start of things that had ended in flames.

"I followed the both of you best I could. After." Lloyd paused, watching as Charlie registered this.

"So you didn't think we were dead, then."

Lloyd's face reddened fiercely as Charlie caught him in the lie. Again Charlie noted the blotches on the man's face, the general impression of, if not illness, then something close to it.

But this curiosity was shoved aside by another thought. Had the son of a bitch still been tracking him? How could he not have known? It felt wrong, off. But if that led him to Emma . . .

Lloyd reached into the breast pocket of his coat, extracting a small photograph. "You aren't always the most subtle of travelers," he said.

Charlie stared. It was the fading photo taken during the war. His smiling image, his arm draped over Robert Worley's shoulder. A mixture of surprise and grief pounded in his chest. "Where did you get this?"

"A smart man doesn't spill all his secrets," Lloyd said. He slid the photo back under his coat before Charlie could make a move to grab it. "I needed to stay one step ahead of them. They've changed names so many times. They pop up here and there, like the fountain itself. They haven't been the Church of Light in a few years. But we're the key. We're like a holy grail of abomination. The possibility of our continued existence is what holds them together. Find us, and they heal the world. Or so the theory goes. Well, I prefer not to be found."

"And yet here you are," Charlie said.

The sun was setting now, and the street lamps were coming on. The wind had shifted, the air clearing. Evening was settling golden over Manhattan. In a few days it would be All Hallows' Eve.

"If you know where Emma is," Charlie began, but

Kingsley Lloyd sucked in a sharp breath, gazing at a point over Charlie's shoulder.

The men advancing toward them were not familiar. Both wore overcoats. One had a wool cap pulled low over his head.

A cold sweat prickled on Charlie's lower back.

The men were striding faster.

"Charlie," said Kingsley Lloyd.

The two men were jogging now, almost to them.

"Emma's dead," Kingsley Lloyd said, panicked. "I don't know how exactly. But I'm sure of it. I—we need to get out of here. They're Walters's followers."

Once during the war, a bomb had exploded close enough to temporarily take out Charlie's hearing. A loud buzzing had filled his head, smoke choking his lungs, his clothes and face splattered with more than one man's blood. He would never know why it hadn't been him. Why others had died and he had remained whole and standing. Every man on those battlefields, every fallen soldier at Verdun and Ypres and Château-Thierry, they'd all had people to come back to. All except Charlie.

But something—fate? Love? He didn't understand it, would never understand it—had saved him again and again and again. Charlie Ryan, who already had the miracle of eternity in his veins, had continued to be a very lucky man.

The man with the wool hat lifted his arm and waved.

Charlie had never in his life been still unless he'd meant to. Now he found himself unable to move. Lloyd shoved his hand back into his pocket, and this time extracted a small black velvet bag. He tossed it into Charlie's hands.

"Emma's dead, Charlie."

Lloyd turned then and then bolted across the street.

"Hey!" the wool-capped man called.

Charlie squared his stance for a fight. But the wool-capped man and his companion ran, right on by Charlie without stopping. Charlie saw now that they had been waving at a woman standing in the doorway of an apartment building. He moved to give chase, only to see Kingsley Lloyd hop onto the running board of a snappy blue Chrysler and motor around the corner.

Now Charlie stood alone in the wind. He stood there for a very long time. Then he opened the velvet bag. His hands were steady despite the tumultuous beating of his heart. In the bag sat the gold-chained pocket watch he'd given Emma. The one he'd had engraved with their names, the one with the sound of the wind and the call of the hawk when you opened it.

Emma watched as Pete struggled to open his eyes. They were swollen, the tender flesh underneath quickly turning purple, a bump the size of a goose egg rising on his forehead. A deep, nasty cut was oozing on his right cheek. Emma, her numb hands and feet tied to her chair, was not in much better condition.

"Where are we?" His voice was hoarse, but he was awake and alive. That was all that mattered.

"Not sure," she said.

"You can do better, O'Neill." Pete twisted in his chair, then groaned. "Shit," he said. "Something's wrong with my arm."

Coral's eyes had drifted closed, and Emma could hear she was breathing unevenly.

Not good. Not at all. They needed to get her—and themselves—out of here.

"What the hell did they hit me with?" Pete grunted. "A cement truck?" He tried to stand, managing to hoist himself and the chair into a C shape. The cut on his cheek dripped blood on the cement floor. He took a labored step then another. He was right. There *was* something wrong with his arm. Or maybe his collarbone.

"Let me come to you," Emma said, struggling to lift herself. "You're in no shape to move."

From the cot, Coral shook with a loud, hacking, wet cough. They were lucky she wasn't already dead.

Emma trudged slowly toward Pete, the heavy chair lashed to her.

On the other side of the warehouse, Coral stopped coughing. "I'm sorry," she said. "This is all my fault. But he was the guy from the bar, you know. The one you left with that night. And there he was waving to me when I went to your school to look for you, so I figured—"

"*Guy* you *left* with?" Pete grunted as he rose and began trekking toward Emma, who was still dragging her chair toward him. "Guy. You. Left. With?"

"It's a long story," Emma grunted back at him.

"We've got time," Pete said.

Emma chose to ignore him.

Coral's voice faded in and out. "I heard them talking. That Matt guy went to meet some med-school friend. The others are gone, I think, but Matt's coming back. He thought I was asleep, I guess, or maybe unconscious. They've been giving me shots of something. And he ran out of it, I think. What's this all about? What's it got to do with you? I'm really scared, Emma. I don't even know how long I've been here. But I think it's awhile. I can smell myself. And it's not a good smell."

Emma tried to smile reassuringly. "You smell fine. And we *are* getting out of here. Don't worry."

She hopped a few more inches toward Pete. Her head was throbbing.

"Stand still, O'Neill," Pete grumbled. "I've got this."

"No, you don't," she said, then swiveled her gaze as best she could to Coral and added, "Detective Mondragon gets cranky when he gets hit on the head."

"I was so stupid," Coral said.

Emma hopped another inch. The chair was weighing her down. "There's a lot of that going around," she said.

"Hugo and I had this huge argument. He thought I didn't love him, and I . . . it was just one of those things, you know? I should have called you. But I just stormed out. Grabbed my keys, and I guess I left my phone on my bed. I was just going to your apartment. But you weren't there. Only I'd gotten it in my head that I had to talk to you. I was just *so pissed* at Hugo. How could he think I'd stop loving him just because we were in a new place? When you love someone like that, it's different, you know?"

Emma *did* know. But this was neither the time nor the place for that conversation.

Pete had reached Emma, and he hopped heavily and spun around to position himself so they were back-to-back. "I'm going to untie your hands, O'Neill, which is possibly against my better judgment right now. And then you're going to untie mine. Got it?"

Emma reached out as best she could with her numb fingers straining for Pete's hands. Then their fingers touched, and she scooted closer as she felt him pulling at the cords.

"Am I going to die?" Coral's voice was breathy and small.

"No," Emma and Pete said together, and the combined impact of this had Coral mumbling, "Okay."

The rope restraining Emma's hands went slack. "You got it," she told Pete. She wiggled her fingers as he freed her other hand, and then she was shaking them at the wrists, trying to get the feeling back.

"I'm good," Pete said hoarsely.

It worried Emma that Matt was still gone, that they were alone, that it wasn't terribly difficult to break free. But she had no time for what-ifs right now.

Coral cleared her throat. "I can't believe I trusted that lying ass. I walked *around* with him, looking for you. I got suspicious when you weren't at the student center like he said you would be, but then he—"

"It's *not* your fault," Emma interrupted, bending to untangle her feet. Her fingers were clumsy, and it wasn't going quickly.

"For God's sake," muttered Pete, "untie me now!"

Coral broke into another coughing fit. "But I thought you liked Matt," she began.

"Nope," Emma said, still bent over trying to free her feet. "And I'm the stupid one. Just so we're clear."

"We're clear," Pete said. "Now get me out of this damn chair. I think my shoulder is broken." He groaned under his breath.

Emma would have complied. Only it was then that she heard the sound of a door sliding open, and Matt, whose last name she had never learned, sauntered back into the warehouse with the pace of a man with no need to hurry.

He looked taller than she remembered him, and less rumpled. She hoped she could do something—anything—before he noticed that her hands, which she slipped back behind her as Matt walked through the door, were no longer tied to the chair. She tucked her feet under the chair.

Matt flicked his gaze slowly around the room, then homed in on her. He tilted his head, and she was annoyed that, he reminded her of one of the hawks that Charlie used to train.

She met his gaze, held it until he blinked. "What did you

inject her with?" She hoped she sounded more commanding than she currently felt.

"Does it matter?" Matt asked. "For the record, I wasn't sure until I went back to your place. But I saw that old pocket watch hanging there and knew I was right. You were Emma. Emma O'Neill. And you had no idea who I was. Not a clue. Although I have to say you can hold your bourbon."

Anger burned in Emma's chest. "More than I can say for you."

She had hated many things over the years, and with good reason, but the thought of him touching Charlie's watch seemed one of the worst. Still, she forced herself to stay where she was. Surely Matt saw that she and Pete were now back-to-back in the middle of the room. But if she worked fast and kept him talking . . .

Keeping her eyes firmly on Matt, Emma reached behind her for Pete, found his hands. "Let Coral go," she said, willing Matt to keep his focus on her. "She's not who you need."

Matt made a *tsk*ing sound. "You know I can't do that, right?"

"Sure you can," Pete muttered. Emma felt his ropes give as she worked her fingers around the knots.

Coral's coughing sounded ragged now. Whatever she'd been infected with was far more than just poison and probably contagious. Maybe airborne. Maybe Emma had been right the first time. Matt wasn't that bright after all.

Work with that, O'Neill, she told herself.

Matt's lips twisted in a small smile. "You know, when I was a boy, I sometimes thought maybe you were just a myth. But here you are. And I'm the one who found you." He stretched out his arms, a move that reminded her of Glen Walters. "The things you must have seen. The places and the people.

Time rolling at your fingertips. And what are you doing with it? Living in some Dallas apartment? Why? You could have anything you wanted. But here you are. What a waste."

"Don't know what you're talking about." Emma's fingers fumbled with another knot. Almost.

"World's a funny place," Matt said. He seemed to have no pressing desire to kill them or move whatever this was forward. Was he just toying with her? Was he waiting for something?

He *had* to be waiting for something. But what? Who? They would have to make their move—*she* would have to make her move—before that something happened.

"Your friend Coral here likes you so much that she posted lovely pictures of you for the whole world to see. Including me."

"And your point is?" Emma tried for casual, bored even. *Get yourself loose, Pete,* she thought. And winced as she heard him groan again in pain.

"It wasn't even that hard to find you," Matt said. "I think that's why I didn't believe it was actually you. Sitting in that dive bar. Eating tacos some girl sold you off the street. Drinking bourbon. The girl detective with a huge secret of her own. Thinking I was just some guy."

Emma rolled her eyes. "Don't overestimate yourself. Those General Patton stories are getting a bit stale, by the way."

"I'm sorry, Emma," Coral said.

Emma could hear the rasp of her breath. She glared at Matt. "She needs a doctor. Just let her go. We can do this on our own."

"I think you're confusing who's in charge here, Emma." Matt placed a hand on his chest. "You know there weren't many of us faithful left when I took over for my father. Guardians of the world, that's what he called us. Destroy the evil. Praise the good. No middle ground. Just right and wrong."

"I think *you've* got that confused," Emma said.

Matt shrugged. "And I think you've got something I want. But you're not the only one, you know?"

Did he mean Charlie? Emma wasn't sure what was faster than galloping, but whatever it was, her heart was doing it.

"I hoped to do this another way," Matt said. "But you can't always get what you want, can you?"

"So you're going with a lame old song lyric?" Emma drawled.

Pete's voice rose from behind her. "Hey, Matt, you know what Patton said, don't you? 'The object of war is not to die for your country but to make the other bastard die for his.'"

She knew his hands were still partially tied, but Emma felt Pete rise. "Go!" he hollered. "Now!"

Chapter Twenty-Two

Emma launched herself from the chair, slamming into Matt, anger and adrenaline surging as her body collided with his.

They hit the floor together, her elbow knocking over a container of something acrid and pungent, sending it puddling just beyond where they sprawled, her forehead smacking the floor with an audible thump.

This time the blackness threatened to drag her under.

"Emma!"

She jerked her head painfully in Pete's direction. His hands might be free, but his legs were still tied to the chair, his left shoulder definitely broken or dislocated. How had he even managed to untie her hands?

In that distracted second, Matt pushed up hard, breaking her hold, and somehow he was dragging her to her feet, the cold metal nose of a gun pushed against the back of her aching head.

"Don't!" Pete said, his voice a low and dangerous growl.

Emma's vision had gone wonky, spots and pinwheels, and a sharp panic rushed over her.

"Let her go," Pete said. "Let both of them go. Deal with me."

Matt tightened his grip on Emma. He pressed his mouth to her ear, and she shuddered. "We're going to walk out this door together, Emma. Just you and me."

The dizziness threatened to overcome her, but she forced her voice to stay steady. "Your friends run off on you?" Because there had been others, so why weren't they here? Had something happened?

"Shut up," Matt said. "Get moving." He was backing toward the door now, dragging her with him, the gun still pressed to her temple.

She was so dizzy it was hard to move. So dizzy that she barely heard the sound of the door opening behind them. And then an excited and oddly high-pitched voice said, "Drop the gun. Do it now."

Matt whipped around, pulling her with him.

"Your friends aren't coming back, by the way," said a short, bow-legged man with distinctly frog-like features. He was wearing tidy khakis, a striped button-down, and what looked to Emma's increasingly hazy vision as some form of boat shoe. Other than his footwear—which was a step more fashionable than the clumsy work boots he had favored in the distant past, he looked exactly as Emma remembered him.

"Kingsley Lloyd?" She wondered if she was hallucinating. How was he here? Why was he here? Was he working with Matt? How was that possible?

But all she could manage was, "You're alive."

She'd known, of course, deep down, that he probably was. But the shock of it—of another person who had traversed the decades, who had lived and lived, even if it was this absurd, traitorous man. Even if it wasn't Charlie. She was shaking now, and not just from the waves of dizziness.

"So are you," Lloyd said, and there was something like wonder or delight in his wide eyes.

"Well, I'll be damned," Pete muttered.

"What the hell did you do?" Matt lifted the gun from her head and waved it over Emma's shoulder at Kingsley Lloyd.

"Evened the odds," said Kingsley Lloyd.

Matt was dragging her again, the gun still pointed at Lloyd. Emma could see Pete now, his gaze flicking from the gun to Emma and Matt to Kingsley Lloyd.

Emma could no longer hear Coral's labored breathing.

It was like that first day she had loved Charlie. The day she had let the hawk free. Emma O'Neill, the girl who could not bear to make mistakes, the girl who would make so many of them that she would soon lose track. She had lost everything but never given up hope. Would never give up as long as her heart was still beating in her chest, because really, what else could she do?

The years pressed on that beating heart, all of them, a tumble of lives and moments, of words said and unsaid, promises made and broken.

And a thought rose from her jumbled brain. If Matt wanted her dead, he would have already shot her. There was no reason not to.

So if not that, then . . .

A memory of something, of one thing, rose to her tongue. Or rather, she allowed it to rise. Because Emma remembered mostly everything. The endless span of days and weeks and months and years.

Yes, Emma thought. It could work. It *had* to work.

She turned her head as best she could. "Do you know we're mostly made of water, Matt? Did Mr. Lloyd tell you that was the key?"

A few feet from her, Kingsley Lloyd made a *hmm* sound in the back of his throat.

"Shut up," said Matt, but she knew he was listening.

"What did he promise you? Eternal life? To be like us? Because that's what you really want, isn't it? I thought you wanted what they've all wanted. To kill me. To make sure no one stayed on this earth longer than they were supposed to. Because that just ruins your fun, doesn't it?"

Matt waved the gun at Lloyd again. "You told me you had something."

Emma pondered his question, but her head was throbbing harder now, and her left eye erupted in some kind of kaleidoscope pattern. The odor of the liquid spilling out of the container made her breath come harder in her chest. She managed a quick glance at Pete. His gaze was locked on Matt's gun.

She shifted her attention to Kingsley Lloyd and saw his lips lift in a quick slash of a smile.

"Do you remember what you asked me that day, Mr. Lloyd? About the lobsters?"

"Lobsters?" Matt yanked Emma tighter against him. Pete's gaze slid to Emma's, and she could see the question in his eyes. *What are you doing?* Even if she had been able to answer, she wasn't sure what she would say.

"They don't age," Emma said aloud. "They just get bigger."

"Enough of this bullshit." Matt's hand steadied on the gun.

"You don't want to kill me," Emma said. "You want to *be* me." When she heard his quick intake of breath, she knew it was the truth. "You want to know what it's like?"

She had him now. She knew it. She just had to distract him long enough for Pete to make a move. And if Emma knew anything, it was that Pete, injured or not, gun or not, *would* make a move.

"It's *amazing*. Like Christmas and birthdays and sunsets over the ocean all rolled into one. I don't age. I don't get sick. Ever. I won't ever contract a cold or the flu. I won't get cancer. I won't start forgetting my keys and discover I've got Alzheimer's. My hair won't go gray. My skin won't wrinkle. I won't wake up one day and think, 'My God, I've wasted all these years, and now I don't have many left.' You know why? Because I've got an infinite number. I won't drop down dead from some aneurysm. If there's a place I haven't seen, well, I can always go see it tomorrow. Because I have *all* the tomorrows. Every single one. You know why? Because Kingsley Lloyd here, he found the impossible. And then he shared it with me."

Emma's head was flying now, threatening to rise dizzily off her shoulders. "What did he promise you, Matt? Was it that?"

Matt's gaze was locked on Kingsley Lloyd. "You said you had it still. The plant."

"I do," Lloyd said. "Absolutely."

Kingsley Lloyd's face did not give away the lie. Did not let on to what he must know just as she did—that the few original sips of tea from the plant on the island was all they had needed. It didn't matter if the stream had disappeared, that none of them (so she assumed) had ever found it again.

She had not aged. Not one bit. And neither, she assumed, had Charlie. Kingsley Lloyd looked exactly as she remembered him, which was to say, not that good. But he was the same, just as she was.

She would always be *this*.

Unless of course, Matt shot her in the head. That she preferred to avoid.

And then Matt's arm jerked and something sharp and hot grazed Emma's cheek, and then Kingsley Lloyd was screaming and swearing and clutching his arm.

In that moment, Pete, chair and broken shoulder and col-larbone and all, hurled himself at her and Matt.

What followed was a wild commotion, a flurry of bodies, and a dropped gun skittering across the floor, but not going off. Emma grabbed for Matt but he twisted away, running for the gun. And then out of the corner of her still-functioning right eye, she saw a flame, just as she heard the rasp of a match striking.

"Go!" Kingsley Lloyd was shouting, pushing her aside. "Go!" He dropped the match to the floor.

The fire caught the spilled liquid from the containers, burned, and spread swiftly across the floor in a mesmerizing line straight toward Matt, who had almost reached the gun.

The flames caught the cuff of his pants, traveling up his leg in the time it took Emma to realize what was happening.

"Pete!" She reached for him, not sure how she had the strength because she was so woozy, but managing to shove him toward the door. Then she somehow scrambled over to Coral, because even in her terror, she knew that whatever Coral was sick with, Emma and Lloyd were the only ones who could safely come near her.

But Lloyd stood where he was, arm dripping blood, a box of wooden matches in his hand.

The room was burning faster now, empty wooden pallets furiously catching on fire, the whole thing igniting.

Had it been Matt who had set that apartment in *her* building on fire? Or Lloyd? Or neither of them? She saw her family and Charlie's, trapped in that room in the Alligator Farm and Museum. She saw them as she and Charlie had found them. Matt was burning to death like they had. Like *she* might have in her apartment, had Pete not knocked on the door.

She watched dizzily as Matt dropped to the floor, rolling, but the flames were everywhere, and he was screaming.

"Help him," she shouted as she untied Coral from the cot. "Help him." The girl's skin was too warm, her fever seeming to build as she leaned heavily on Emma. "Help him."

But no one did, and Emma would always know that a part of her felt it was a fair exchange for everything else. Whatever Matt was, whatever he wanted, whatever he understood in those moments, she would never know. He had not told them. He hadn't said he was sorry or threatened revenge. He hadn't explained himself beyond the actions that he had already committed.

Emma saw her parents' faces. Her brothers and sister. Simon. His hair.

"O'Neill!" Pete stumbled to her side, barely mobile, somehow unbound from the chair. "Keep moving. Don't you dare give up now."

The insistence of his voice broke her fear. "Don't touch Coral," she rasped, the smoke filling her lungs. "She's too contagious. I'll get her out of here. Help him. We can't let him burn."

"It's too late," said Kingsley Lloyd. Emma registered that Matt was no longer screaming.

Lloyd pushed on the door. There was a rush of air, and the flames were growing, but she was outside and not on fire.

Could they have saved Matt? She didn't know. What did she really know, anyway? After all this time, not enough. Never enough.

KINGSLEY LLOYD WAS bleeding, and Pete was broken, and Emma—still and always seventeen—had saved Coral Ballard. She had told Matt what she thought he wanted to believe.

She thought of that tattoo on his arm.

Whatever he'd actually believed hadn't saved him.

Now she sat on the cold, weed-strewn ground in the middle of what was clearly some half-abandoned warehouse district. She saw the shadow of downtown Dallas looming in the distance, and wondered vaguely if Matt had wanted to die, to become a martyr, if the fire was a surprise or the plan all along. But there was nothing that could be done. The warehouse was an inferno.

In the distance and growing closer, the sound of sirens and emergency vehicles filled the air.

"Stupid bastard," said Kingsley Lloyd.

Chapter Twenty-Three

Kingsley Lloyd had always known he was destined for greatness. Even before. The problem was, no one else knew it. Even more, no one cared. His life was a sham, but the funny thing was, sometimes even a sham turns out to be the truth.

When he arrived in St. Augustine, Florida, on a hot April afternoon, the sun beating down relentlessly, even with the cooling ocean breeze sifting over him, he was almost dead broke, without any family relations he cared to claim, and unclear why he'd chosen this place. He was on the run from the law after a slight altercation concerning his organizational role in the type of questionable financial pyramid that would later be referred to as a Ponzi scheme.

Kingsley Lloyd—whose real name was something else he had sloughed off so long ago, he barely remembered it—was moderately educated, although the best and most important things he knew he had taught himself through reading, by pissing people off, and by observing with great interest all he aspired to yet hadn't found a way to acquire.

In shorter terms, a con man, although not always a successful one.

But he was, as he would later see in Emma and Charlie, and the late Frank Ryan, ever hopeful and optimistic that things would turn around. He knew when he stumbled out of that warehouse many years later that, had he asked her, Emma would have said she was none of those things, that she was instead, jaded and cynical and terribly lonely. He would have told her he could do nothing about the last one, but the fact that she continued to search and live and figure things out made her far more positive-thinking than she acknowledged.

But he also knew she would never ask. She was most likely far too busy mourning the fiery demise of Matthew Thigpen, even though she would eventually realize as Lloyd had, that his death meant they were free. The Church of Light, or the Light Givers as they had renamed themselves, would fracture and dissipate, and eventually some new awful thing might take their place, but for now the threat was gone.

Kingsley Lloyd had done what he'd needed to in order to save his own skin. He'd saved Emma O'Neill, too, or at least that's how he saw it. He figured he owed it to her, although in truth, he rarely thought in those types of terms. He didn't owe anyone anything. He was a survivor.

That—more than any potion of immortality—was what had kept him alive all these years.

When he arrived in St. Augustine, he knew enough natural science and biology and botany and the stray smattering of zoology to offer himself up to the Ryans and O'Neills as an expert herpetologist. The truth was, he had overheard Frank's bragging tales. One con man would protect another, he figured, at least as long as Kingsley Lloyd kept his nose

*clean and did what they were paying him for, or faked it
enough to get by. It all came down to wanting a piece of the
business. Just like he told Charlie that day in 1939 when,
having tracked Charlie down through the army photograph,
he hoped to convince him that Emma was dead.*

*Because if the boy stopped looking for Emma, he would
stay put, and the Light Givers would find him and kill him.
It would be one more safety measure to make sure they never
got to Lloyd. That's how he had worked it out in his head.
Besides, the girl had to be dead by now, didn't she?*

*He'd tried to track both of them, but only Charlie had
left a large enough trail, although Lloyd supposed that was
on purpose. If he had a girl he loved (he'd never quite given
up that possibility, but it no longer seemed likely), he would
have left a set of obvious clues to draw people off her path,
too. So he got it. He really did.*

*Still Charlie Ryan was, in Kingsley Lloyd's estimation, a
romantically deluded fool. He was searching for a ghost.*

*But Emma, well, Glen Walters hadn't found her, but
Lloyd suspected Norman Thigpen had. Or would, if Charlie was right, which seemed unlikely. Still, odder things had
happened. Certainly their eternal life was proof of that. The
key was to make Charlie believe it, to accept that Emma was
dead and gone, regardless of the truth.*

*But that was in 1939. Back when this whole thing began,
back in St. Augustine, the twentieth century brand spanking
new, Lloyd's only thought had been that Florida seemed as
good a place as any to succeed.*

*If that didn't work, he figured he'd make his way across
the country to that other coast. Maybe live in Hollywood out
in California. Get a job in the movie picture industry, because
if there was ever a con man's game, that was it. If Lloyd knew*

anything, it was how to make people believe in dreams and sleight of hand.

But he'd try this first. See what he could make of it.

Kingsley Lloyd had never seen an alligator up close, but why should that stop him? He'd read about them and studied their physiology. It would be enough. Besides, O'Neill and Ryan were self-made men, both of them, which Kingsley admired. Hadn't O'Neill told him straight up that he'd apprenticed for only six months with the former owner when he bought the place? That was how it worked in America. You took what you wanted and hoped for the best. Then you worked your ass off to keep it.

Lloyd was fine with that. The gators scared him, he had to admit. But what was a little fear when he was going to earn his fortune? Be like the Rockefellers or the Hearsts. He could have his own castle someday if he wanted. Nothing was impossible!

He had never imagined the plant at the edge of the now missing pond held the secret to eternity: the plant and the pond together, in concert. He simply thought the plant looked like something he'd read about in an old botany book, one he'd bought in a little odds-and-ends shop on Royal Street in New Orleans. Now there was a strange, magical town, filled with people who believed absolutely in the unseen and the impossible. But oh, the heat. Made Florida feel positively moderate some days.

What he figured was that his little ground-plant concoction might very well stave off that horrid polio virus. The rest of it he watched unfold along with the others, the only difference being, he understood before the rest of them what seemed to be happening. It took the young ones not changing for him to see it.

The ones who weren't like him, already sicker than he cared to admit, had some liver ailment, the doctor had said. It wouldn't kill him right off, but eventually . . .

And then Kingsley Lloyd unwittingly discovered the goddamn, authentic Fountain of Youth.

The rest of it unfurled out of his control.

He felt bad about that, he truly did. He also knew he was lying to himself. He could have told them when he suspected. He could have warned them any number of times about any number of things.

But Kingsley Lloyd was a pragmatic sort. His own skin— even sallow and waxy with that damn liver disease—came first. Successful self-made men prided themselves on seeing opportunities when they arose rather than trying to shoehorn destiny into man-made plans.

So he waited. He watched. He ran when he realized that none of them were a match for the zealotry of Glen Walters and his Church of Light followers. At least the bastards weren't blowing up airplanes or shooting journalists or burning people at the stake. Although you just never knew, did you? Lynch mobs were generally made of one's neighbors.

Case in point, the fire at the museum back in Florida. Case in point, the needless deaths of everyone Charlie and Emma loved. Kingsley Lloyd was still not sure who set the blaze that day, who locked those lovely people in, believing that their deaths would make the world a better place or maybe just ensure the perpetrators a better seat in heaven. In the end, it didn't really matter.

As he tried to tell Emma the day they talked about the lobsters, there was nothing new about hatred or fear or greed or even the human desire to make a permanent mark on the world. Everyone wanted fame and fortune, and those who said they didn't were deluded or liars or both.

Later, he would add to this theory, having spent enough hours watching both CNN *and* America's Got Talent *to come to the unsurprising conclusion that Americans in particular snookered themselves into believing they were above the fray, when in truth, they were just distracted by cheap gas, all-you-can-eat buffets, and a wide variety of made-in-China-sweatshop tchotchkes at Walmart.*

Most people, as Kingsley Lloyd saw it, were one shopping spree away from suicide bombings; they just refused to admit it. Occasionally, they slipped up and gunned down schoolchildren and people in movie theaters and ex-wives. But this tended to happen in the suburbs, where people paid less attention.

He knew that neither Emma nor Charlie would have pegged him for a philosopher. Or that underneath his ugly exterior (yes, he knew what people saw when they looked at him), beat the mostly immortal heart of a philanthropist. A hopeful, optimistic one at that.

Even if immortality meant that whatever he had wouldn't kill him, but he would have to drag it with him through eternity. Such was life. A long one, he hoped.

That he'd chosen to briefly align himself with the man named Matthew Thigpen was another issue entirely. Keeping your enemies closer was part of it. Finding Emma O'Neill was the other part, not that she'd have believed him.

He felt bad about so many things, really, including having tossed that copy of the pocket watch at Charlie that day in New York. But he didn't regret it. He'd known it might come to that. And he was proven right, wasn't he? He had been smart to make copies of all the little things that mattered to the O'Neills and Ryans. He'd crept around both of their houses when the families were out, documenting in detail everything they held precious. He knew this was a cheat, a fraud, but precious items could be used as levers, as buttons, as marionette strings. He knew Charlie would stop running if he thought his beloved was dead.

That was his method. He knew no other way.

Sometimes you do things and you're not even sure why, just that later, you'll need it.

A man did what a man had to do to stay alive. Some tricks were more dangerous than others.

But like any good con man, Kingsley Lloyd was a keen fan of risk.

Risk meant survival. In the end, that was all that mattered.

Lloyd couldn't make up for all that had happened since the day he found that Fountain of Youth, but lighting Matthew Thigpen on fire was a start at justice.

Thigpen had risked and lost. It was, Kingsley Lloyd thought as he hustled from the warehouse, simply the way of the world.

Chapter Twenty-Four

Only later, much later, would Emma piece together the truth—at least most of it—about Matt. Some of it Lloyd himself had told her at the warehouse. The rest she would find out on her own.

Matthew Douglas Thigpen, son of Thomas Paul Thigpen, grandson of Samuel Wade Thigpen, great-grandson of Norman Woolsey Thigpen—himself the heir apparent to a crazy man named Glen Walters—had grown up amidst secrets. The Church of Light, having long ago renamed itself the Light Givers, a private moniker which was perhaps no less ironic given their propensity for killing people in the name of heaven, had not actively preached their word since that tent-revival-turned-murder back in Alabama so many years ago. The one that ended with the death of a girl they thought might be Emma. But this did not mean they had disappeared. To the contrary, they had grown stronger and firmer in their beliefs.

Finding and destroying Emma O'Neill and Charlie Ryan was a cornerstone. But by the time Matt Thigpen arrived in the wide world, the Light Givers—the leadership of which would eventually pass to him—had failed to achieve that task for close to a century. It had become, as Matt had told her half-jokingly, the stuff of legend, words and promises that amounted to nothing substantial. Faith is built on that we cannot see, but faith without noticeable result—well, it can lose its punch after a while.

This was the state of the family business the week after Matthew Thigpen graduated from Vanderbilt with a degree in economics. He came home to his father's compound—a private plot of land not far from Celebration, Florida, a master-planned town created by the Disney corporation. What better place to hide his father's strange and powerful empire than in the Southern-themed, middle-class track-home shadow of the happiest place on earth?

He was well-educated in business matters, enthusiastic and driven, sporting a fresh BELIEVE *tattoo and a fondness for biscuits, country music, and small-batch Tennessee whiskey.*

The good thing, as Matt Thigpen saw it the day his father suffered a massive stroke and died on the spot—lingering only long enough to fix one shocked bright blue eye on his son as if to say, "Well, damn it, I wasn't expecting that"— was that people had short memories. Sports heroes could beat their wives and still end up with one-man shows on Broadway. Gaggles of celebrities tweeted #bringbackourgirls to help save two hundred kidnapped Nigerian school girls, and then seemingly forgot about them, barely noticing when they remained in the hands of the men who had taken them. And that was just the tip of the societal iceberg.

All Matt Thigpen had to do was to tell the true believers now under his leadership that he had found a way to succeed. If you said something often enough, made enough noise, it became the truth. Like the antigluten movement. Or those nutjobs who didn't think kids should be vaccinated. "Real-life clickbait" was how Matt saw it. Matthew Thigpen was a modern boy who thought in those type of metaphors, and so far it had kept him on top of things.

But destiny is a funny thing. Imagine Matt Thigpen's surprise when he stumbled upon a man named Kingsley Lloyd—not only because he was searching for him (it was Matt who had informed the leadership that he suspected that a third immortal was roaming the earth, and that if they found him, he would lead them to the others), but also because Lloyd, ever the pragmatist, had also been tracking Emma in hopes to stay one step ahead of those who wanted to nab her. Like Emma surfacing now and then, this had made Kingsley Lloyd noticeable—unlike Charlie Ryan, who in recent years, had proved much slipperier prey. He was out there, though, Matt thought. It was only a matter of time.

Of course, the string of dead and kidnapped girls had possibly been overkill, so to speak. But this was the plan of action he'd inherited, so what could he do? It had brought Emma out in the open (if only by sparking her friendship with Coral Ballard, who had unwittingly posted pictures of her new friend on her various social sites and thus set off every hopeful Light Giver alarm that hey, this might be it!), but it had spooked Kingsley Lloyd, and now Matthew Thigpen had a mess on his hands.

And then there was his odd burst of conflicted feelings about this girl—woman—whatever she was, who was so many more things than the mere symbol of everything he'd been raised to despise. What he'd felt when he'd held her hand, when he'd kissed her—it was nothing *like what he'd expected. She* was *nothing like what he expected. She was*

pretty—beautiful, really—and funny and clever and smart
. . . and very sad underneath it all. He'd pressed his lips to
hers and had somehow felt the terrible loss and grief and
loneliness that sat just under her skin.

An odd shock to find that Emma O'Neill—despite
her immortal condition that was an abomination to be
destroyed—was human after all.

This was the situation as Matt saw it in the warehouse,
where he stood wondering what the hell he was going to
do with Emma, Coral Ballard, and the detective Pete Mondragon, whom he hadn't expected to be in the thick of things.

And that he had thought himself slick enough to manipu-
late Kingsley Lloyd into helping him while still planning on
killing the little man at some point, well, that had been quite
the error in judgment.

However much Matthew Thigpen believed, *the truth of*
the matter was that the idea of having his own eternal life
drew him like a moth to a flame. And Kingsley Lloyd, that
creepy bastard, had promised him the solution to that.

This was the trouble with believing things for so very
long. Even when you learned that the entire basis for everything that had driven you and made you was a lie, what
could you do?

Matt wanted to believe he did not have—that none of
them had—only one destiny. That he was more than the sum
total of his errors or his genetic lottery, that there were roads
and roads of possibilities stretching in front of him.

But a man would have to live forever for that, wouldn't
he? It was just so damn unfair, he thought as the first licks of
flame caught on his clothes and he began to burn. Life was
too short for all but those immortal few, and now he was lit
like a candle.

The pain and terror consumed him, the shock of what was happening not enough to numb him. Was he dying? Was he even screaming anymore? He didn't know.

Like the doomed Titanic, *sometimes you foolishly stay your course. Matthew Thigpen had stayed his, and now it was burning him alive.*

Chapter Twenty-Five

If Coral had questions about the strange things that had happened, including with Kingsley Lloyd, she was keeping them to herself.

Recovering from both malaria and diphtheria and what seemed to be a touch of dengue fever (the doctors were flabbergasted, and the police detectives vowed to get to the bottom of this, which Emma knew they most certainly *would not*), was enough for her to worry about.

Hugo and her parents stayed by her bedside, or at least as close as the doctors and nursing staff allowed.

"Thank you," Hugo told Emma over and over, hugging her so hard that she couldn't breathe. "Thank you."

"I told you I'd find her," she said, faking a confidence she had never felt. "I'm sorry I didn't get there faster."

The police were dealing with Matt's death and the fire in the warehouse and tracking down anyone else who had been involved with Coral's kidnapping. No one mentioned a connection to the Elodie Callahan case, at least not anyone official. There was security camera footage that while staticky and from an odd angle, showed a sufficient view of Emma and Pete being attacked and hustled into a van, although the faces of the attackers were not visible.

The official conclusion was that Matt, or whoever he was working with, had also set the fire in Emma's apartment building.

The press was having a fine time of it: a detective from New Mexico and a twenty-one-year-old PI no one had ever heard of had solved the abduction of Coral Ballard, even saving the girl.

There was no talk of an odd-looking man named Kingsley Lloyd who had set the fire and then escaped in the commotion of ambulances and cop cars and news vehicles that followed.

There was no mention of the Church of Light, although many theories rose to explain the kidnappings and the fire. Gang violence. Serial killers. A prominent Dallas criminal psychologist made the rounds of the news shows, discussing with spirited enthusiasm the idea that serial killers, although typically loners, could be induced by the violence in popular culture to work in pairs.

Matthew Thigpen had left few clues as to who he really was and what he'd been trying for. He had a sales job at a local furniture store, where he'd worked steadily for the past six months. He hung out at the bar where Emma had met him— enough that the regulars recognized his name and picture.

But there was little else about him, and Emma suspected that the cops would let things slide. He was dead. No living parents. No local friends who came forth. No significant other that anyone could find. A distant cousin in Wichita Falls had come to claim the body and arrange for burial.

In an unrelated story, two men were found dead in another nearby empty warehouse. Drug deal gone bad, it looked like.

They were identified through their fingerprints as Chase Richardson and Travis Lovelace. Both had done jail time in Florida for a variety of small crimes. How and why they were in Dallas in a rundown warehouse sitting in the shadow of the downtown skyline was something the cops had yet to figure out.

Emma knew there were more out there—these people who wanted her dead or wanted what she was. The danger would never truly be over. But for now, she could breathe.

"You think Lloyd will surface again?" Pete asked her the next day.

"Once every hundred years whether he needs to or not," Emma quipped, her tone many degrees lighter than she felt.

She was sitting on a chair next to Pete's hospital bed, waiting for the doctors to release him. Fractured shoulder. Dislocated collarbone. Contusions on the face and neck. No surgery, but he'd be wearing a sporty blue sling for the next few weeks until everything healed.

Her own head felt like she'd been hit by a truck: a huge shiner under one eye, a minor concussion, and a couple of nice knots still rising from the back of her head under her hair. An abrasion where the bullet from Matt's gun had grazed her cheek. It was all healing fast, but it hurt like hell, nonetheless.

There was so much Emma wanted to ask Kingsley Lloyd. So much he might know that she could use. Why had he promised Matt immortality? Did he know something—anything—about Charlie?

Lloyd was the one to set the fire that had killed Matt. She had pegged him as many things long ago, but a killer hadn't been one of them. Still, people changed. The world changed.

Only Emma had remained the same—physically, at any rate. Once the bruises healed.

She told herself that, really, she was no worse off than

she had been. In fact, better now that, at least for the time being, the murders had stopped. She could sink back under the radar. Move on. Start over. It would be okay.

But it wasn't okay. Not at all.

"You stopped the bad guys," Pete said and reached for her hand, squeezing gently. It was a vast oversimplification.

"Maybe."

Pete kicked back the covers and, with a low grunt, eased himself up. He was paler than she liked to see, and not just because of the white and blue hospital gown, his thin face even gaunter today. She hated that this was her fault, although she knew he would say it wasn't.

"O'Neill."

She raised an eyebrow.

"Girls were dying. Now they're not. I say you did what you set out to do."

Emma shrugged.

A steady rain was beating against the outside window. The day was gray and bleak. Outside Pete's room, the nursing staff bustled back and forth.

"Em," said Pete after a bit, "you could come back to Albuquerque with me. Bunk in my spare room till you found a place. Partner up, even. If you want to."

In her aching head she was already thinking that, really, it would be better for both of them if she just moved on and didn't look back.

"Green chile cheeseburgers," he added encouragingly, and she laughed, just a little.

"I'll think about it."

His gaze lingered. "He'd be proud of you, you know. Your Charlie. I wish he could see what you've become."

"You don't know what I was," she said and knew this

sounded both fierce and cruel. But he *didn't* know. Most days, she felt *she* didn't, either.

Emma walked out of the room then, telling him she'd be back. In the empty waiting area, she curled up in a chair by the window and allowed herself to cry.

She wasn't sure how long she'd been sitting there—just five minutes or so—when she felt rather than heard someone else come into the small room.

Kingsley Lloyd, a wool cap pulled low over his head, wearing a navy nylon zip-up jacket that seemed totally incongruous with the man she remembered, was standing next to her chair, a pained expression on his frog-like face.

Emma's heart surged hopefully. Why would he come back now, if not to tell her about Charlie? That was the only reason she could think of.

But Emma was Emma. Or at least, as Pete had just reminded her, she was the Emma she had become.

"You lit him on fire," she said, although she supposed Lloyd would argue that he had simply dropped a match. In her head, she saw Matt Thigpen burning.

Lloyd shrugged. "He would have killed you, Emma. Not to make too fine of a point of it."

"Is that how you justify things these days? Then I guess I haven't missed much in a hundred years."

"The men who came before him killed your family a hundred years ago, Miss O'Neill."

"Old news."

They stared at each other. She waited. When his gaze tightened, Emma's heart lurched again, but not in a good way.

"He's dead," Kingsley Lloyd said, and for a few grateful seconds, Emma thought he meant Matt. "He's been dead for a long while."

Everything inside Emma felt as though it crumbled to dust. Her breath stopped. Her heart paused midbeat. If she could have died because of these things, she would have.

"I don't believe you."

He slid his hand into his pocket and pulled out a yellowing photograph.

Charlie. Her Charlie. Wearing a uniform and posing with some other soldiers—no, pilots, because there was an airplane behind them. So pilots, yes. He had flown, then. Just like he always wanted to. Emma was breathing again, heaving gulps, trying to grasp the truth.

Lloyd reached back into his pocket and handed her something else: a fragile piece of paper. A telegram announcing the death of Charlie Ryan, RAF pilot, shot down over France on April 22, 1917.

"You can look it up," Lloyd said. "Verify it. I imagine you will. I'm sorry to be the one to tell you. I'm sorry I've known and you haven't. But it's the truth, Emma, and I decided you needed to know."

She wouldn't allow him the satisfaction of seeing her destroyed. She didn't know what his end game was, but with a man like that, it was always something.

"Go the hell away before I call the cops," she said, as though this was a threat. They both knew it wasn't. But they both knew she was capable of more than she was showing.

Something in his face told her he hadn't planned on giving her the photograph. But he held it out now, and she took it, slowly as though it didn't mean much, the aging paper sliding against her fingertips, her heart beating hard as she held this piece of Charlie. She didn't have to look at it again, although she knew she would. The image—each curve and line of his face, his body, the slip of a smile on his face—was already carved into her memory.

Lloyd finally turned and walked away, boots slapping the hospital tile, and when he was out of sight, she ripped the telegram into tiny shreds and sprinkled them over the garbage can by the water fountain.

She did not cry again. Not then.

Instead, she walked back to Room 358 and told Pete that she would go with him to New Mexico.

She had watched a man burn to death.

It was enough tragedy for one week.

Chapter Twenty-Six

Dallas, Texas

Present

Kingsley Lloyd drove west out of Dallas on I-30 heading toward Fort Worth. From there he would cut north, skirting Oklahoma, angling through New Mexico and up through Colorado toward Wyoming. He wasn't exactly sure what he would do when he arrived, but he'd recently purchased a bit of land and a trailer outside of Cody, not far from the Grand Tetons. Beautiful country. A good place to start over.

He was fond of the West, although he'd been through much of the wide world and loved many of its more obscure little corners. A café in Istanbul that served the most amazing Turkish coffee. A pizza place in Dublin, where he'd once tracked Charlie but hadn't made contact. A lake house he'd rented for a year on Lake Superior. He'd loved listening to the boats and foghorns. A diner on the west side of Chicago, where Emma had briefly worked before the Church of Light had murdered Eddie Higgins and sent her running again.

She'd been easy to find that time, although not after that. Emma was good at sliding beneath the surface of things, which he admired. The boy—Charlie—Lloyd had found him, too, all those years ago. And now Matthew Thigpen, well, that hadn't been easy, but he'd figured it out and understood the man's weaknesses. If you are going to stay alive in this world, you have to know how to get one over on the other guy.

Sometimes he had searched for the fountain. If it existed once, it would exist again. Maybe if he found it, he could find a way to cure his illness. He told himself it was just a matter of time before he found the right place. And time was something Kingsley Lloyd hoped to have a lot of.

He had not imagined himself a man who could set another man on fire, but self-preservation was simply science. Survival of the species and all that.

Killing Matthew Thigpen was in its own way no different than giving Charlie Ryan the copy of the pocket watch or showing him that same picture he had shown Emma. You threw people off their game, introduced a sleight of hand, made them doubt, and while they collected themselves, you moved on.

He had kept himself from being the target. That was all that mattered.

He liked Emma O'Neill. He always had. Such a smart girl. In other circumstances, he might have suggested joining forces. Her face when he had handed her that picture—it had made him sad. But he had to make sure she stopped searching once and for all. Let the dead rest and the Church of Light, whatever was left of it, believe that there was no one else to find. No man named Kingsley Lloyd who held the secret to eternity.

Besides, Charlie Ryan had to be dead by now. Thigpen had hinted at it, and although Lloyd wasn't sure, it seemed likely.

Either way, he was free. He was alive. Still and always, which was just fine with him. It was a big country, America. Still a lot of empty spaces.

Yes, *he thought as he watched the sun dipping below the horizon, huge and red and brilliant. Yes.*

Chapter Twenty-Seven

It wasn't that Charlie Ryan had ever stopped searching. It was simply that he had never found her. No matter where he had gone, no matter how many places, how many times he felt he must have just missed her, there had been no Emma at the end of the day. Or week. Or month. Or year. Just the pain of remembering what had been.

Maybe Kingsley Lloyd had told him the truth. Or maybe in his anger and grief, his belief that he deserved to lose her because he'd foolishly let her go, he'd wandered so far, fought so many battles, reimagined himself so many times, that he had simply lost his way. The pocket watch Lloyd had tossed to him was a fake, of course. Lloyd had barely disappeared around that New York corner before Charlie saw that.

The serial number was wrong and the sound of the hawk was harsh and discordant. But sometimes, he'd look at the thing anyway, trace his finger across the etched "Emma and Charlie" on the back, and wonder. Where was she? Did she miss him as much as he missed her?

Had she forgiven him for that day he left her? He would

always be seventeen, but he was not the same person he had been then. At least that's what he told himself.

Charlie roamed the world, trying not to overstay his welcome. One time in Chilton, Texas, he enrolled himself in high school, concocting a story about a traveling father in the oil business who'd sent him to live with a recluse aunt. He stayed on for a few years after that, working at a local ranch, foolishly indulging the need to be the boy and then the young man he had left behind so long ago. Until the rumors started. Where was this aunt of his? And this boy wonder football player who never looked a day over seventeen—how come he still looked like a kid?

Charlie knew too well what could come of that type of notoriety. Plus you never knew. Even in this small town, someone could be related to someone else who, back down the line, had lived in Florida at the turn of the twentieth century.

But sometimes he couldn't help himself because always he hoped that Emma would see or hear. A strange tightrope walk, balancing hiding while still surfacing enough that she could find him even as he was always trying to find her.

He picked up and moved on not long after he'd heard those comments from the checker at the Quick Mart on Route 7.

There were tricks he'd learned to stay invisible, and if Emma was alive, he was sure she'd learned them, too. Ways to fake social security numbers and get bank accounts and keep to yourself. It wasn't as hard as one would imagine. Like anything else, you just got used to it.

Once in Chicago, he knew he'd been close. He'd read about a murder of a boy, and when he looked at the picture in the paper, it was like looking at himself. There had been an Emma Ryan registered at that high school. He knew it was her. He knew it. But she was gone. No trace.

He flew those crop dusters, and then in the '50s, he gave in and was hired on as a daredevil pilot in a small traveling air show. The spectators loved him, photographers snapping pictures as he barrel-rolled the tiny plane and made billows of white smoke plumes in the blue sky. He was Charlie Murray then. Maybe one day, one of those people staring up at him would be Emma.

"Some guys came around asking questions about a Charlie Ryan," Ernie Anderson, who ran the show, told him one day. They were doing a series of appearances outside small towns in Missouri and Illinois and Iowa.

Charlie packed up his gear and headed out before the next show.

He stopped flying after that, slipping below the radar and keeping to himself.

Over the years, Charlie felt as though he was arriving just seconds after Emma left. A phantom sense, as though he'd lost a limb but still searched for it, still felt the ache.

After that there came a series of journeys that led him to a place and a life that made sense. That was more than a placeholder but less than what he wanted. He thought he was perhaps making his late father proud. And Emma, too, because he remembered that first moment he'd noticed her, the hawk on his arm, eyes fast on this girl who would steal his heart even before he understood what it was to love someone.

And here he was now, tying a band gently around the ankle of a snow eagle at the tribal aviary where he'd come to live and work. He had never discovered the truth or the lie about his Calusa ancestors, but he felt the connection, anyway. Or at least the private joke. A Calusa had shot that damn Juan Ponce de León in the leg with a poison arrow, causing his untimely demise. It seemed a fitting metaphor for Charlie's extensive and colorful life.

Charlie Ryan had talent when it came to taking care of wild things. He had, after all, been at it for a very long time. So the tribal council had given him a job.

It was later in the evening than he normally worked, but the bird had come recently to the refuge, and Charlie was the one who best knew what to do with it. He was, in any case, feeling sentimental. He'd been here in this place up past Oklahoma City for three years, and it was almost time to move on. The eternal problem of his existence.

A tiny town, with one stoplight and two restaurants, one a Mexican café, the other a diner that doubled as a washateria on the other side. The café had a bar—two beers on tap—and so that's where he went.

He ordered a Budweiser. He was drinking it around 10:30 P.M. when he turned his attention to the ancient television sagging from the ceiling. A story from down in Texas (Dallas was only four hours south) had made one of the national news channels. A murder case. And a kidnapping. There'd been a spate of those, he knew. But hadn't there always been? Charlie never ceased to wonder at the twenty-four-hour news cycle. So much repetition and invention of crisis where only a minor bobble really existed.

He sipped the Bud and munched a chip or two from the bowl the bartender—her name was Amy, and she lived a few miles up the road with her little boy Sammy—had set in front of him.

"You want to order some food?" Amy asked him. "Before the kitchen closes?"

He didn't answer her. In fact, the glass slipped from his hand and hit the bar with a clunk, tipping over and spilling the last of the beer onto the rough wooden surface.

Unless he was mistaken, the news piece showed Emma O'Neill, looking as she always had, walking out of some hospital, where she had been taken after helping rescue a girl who'd been kidnapped. There was more to the story, but he missed it.

Charlie was already up and running, grabbing his keys, cranking the ignition in his pickup, heading for Dallas. Hands on the wheel, eyes on the horizon, he felt the ties of all the things that had held him earthbound for so long loosening.

Driving toward Emma—it had to be Emma—felt like flying.

Chapter Twenty-Eight

Peter Mondragon was packing up his truck, a stubborn man who insisted that he was just fine with one good arm. Fortunately, Emma O'Neill traveled light, almost as light as he did. He was glad she was coming back to Albuquerque with him. It might not be the life she wanted, but it was a good place, a solid city at the edge of the mountains—not as green or lush as some places, but fine enough.

He was tired of police work—of the politics and the infighting. If he hung up his own PI shingle, she could partner with him. They made a damn good team. He just needed to remember not to act all fatherly with her. Emma O'Neill needed a business partner, not a parent.

He tossed his duffel bag into the back, wincing as the motion tugged at his dislocated shoulder even though he was using the other arm, and laughed aloud. Emma was decades older than he was. But in this business, it was good to have someone watching out for you. For both of them.

Emma hadn't explained why she'd suddenly changed her mind about coming with him, but he suspected she'd tell him eventually. That's how it was between them. Keeping Emma O'Neill's secrets meant not pushing until she was ready.

If he'd been a drinking man still, he'd have cracked open a beer and toasted to new beginnings. But Pete hadn't been a drinking man in over a decade. Not since he'd screwed up his marriage and sunk his career back in San Francisco and lit out for the desert and the mountains and the clear-headedness that came with taking things one day at a time.

He'd told Emma most of it. Hadn't told her what he'd been contemplating right before he worked that murder case and she somehow appeared, and then there they were, elbow to elbow in clues. Things had changed after that.

He knew she thought she had never made a difference, that her long tenure—he still had trouble wrapping his brain around it sometimes, even though he knew it was God's absolute truth—had produced nothing of lasting value. That's why he'd told her what he had earlier today.

He didn't know if it would stick in that thick O'Neill skull. But it might. Time would tell. She'd be okay if no more crazy cults went after her and tried to burn her to death or kidnapped her friends and injected them with poison and diseases or whatever other crap they came up with. One thing was for sure: Emma O'Neill was like a lightning rod for weirdness, for the dark things that most people never saw. But Pete imagined that came with immortal territory.

And then he laughed again that he had a life in which that sentence was even possible.

Would she ever find this Charlie Ryan? It seemed impossible at this point. A hundred years! Pete couldn't imagine searching for his ex-wife for a hundred years. But his own failings aside, Shawna had not been the love of the ages. He had loved her, yes. She had, as far as he knew, loved him. But to search for her for a century? He'd have to have his own thick head examined.

But Emma, well, that was another story. There was no one else like Emma O'Neill. Maybe that was a good thing.

As for this fountain thing, he wasn't sure what to make of that, either. If Emma said it still existed somewhere, then he believed her. Would he partake of it if she discovered its location during his lifetime? He had no damn idea. But if Pete had learned one thing since meeting Emma, it was that stranger things had happened. Would continue to happen. And somehow he was smack in the middle of them.

He had thought, once upon a time, that as a cop he'd seen everything. Well, that was a damn lie, now, wasn't it?

This is what Pete Mondragon was contemplating as he locked up the Tundra and turned to see a mud-streaked blue Ford F-150, riding slowly down Emma's street, like maybe the driver was looking for an address.

Chapter Twenty-Nine

Emma hadn't found the Fountain of Youth again. She hadn't gotten rid of the pesky problem known as Kingsley Lloyd or slain the dragon known as the Church of Light, the crazy cult that was somehow also immortal in its own way. She'd saved a life and been too late to save some others. People she loved with all her heart were dead, and she had never stopped feeling like she should have been able to stop it. In a few minutes she would climb into Pete's oversized truck and head back to New Mexico.

Emma O'Neill had done many things over many decades. Sometimes she felt she could barely remember it all. Much of it had been sad. An equal amount hadn't. Her hair was still long and brown and wavy. Her eyes were still bright. Her skin flawless. She was still impatient and ever on the move. She loved art and poetry and music. She was a dreamer and pragmatist. She liked vanilla cake with lemon filling and roast chicken and green chile cheeseburgers and pancakes and ridiculously spicy Fritos. She had a huge heart and a quick mind.

Mostly she loved a boy named Charlie Ryan for whom she would never stop searching. And now her heart was breaking—no it *was* broken, shattered—because what had all that been for?

"It could be our first order of business if you want," Pete had said. "Looking for him again." He'd swallowed the last bite of glazed donut he'd brought back when he went out to gas up the truck, washing it down with a huge gulp of coffee. If they did become partners, Emma decided, she'd have to rethink their eating habits. But no, she told him, finding Charlie Ryan would not be part of the deal.

She was folding clothes into a small suitcase. *I'm really doing this*, she thought. She had said her goodbyes to Coral and Hugo, telling them she was going to be working with Pete. She would call, she promised, and at least for a while, she knew she would. Coral would recover, but slowly and maybe not in all ways. Emma felt responsible for that, too.

But she told herself to press forward.

It felt strange, making a move to be with someone rather than hiding. The picture of Charlie was tucked in this case, beneath her clothes. When she got settled in New Mexico, when she had her own place again, she'd find a spot for it. A frame, she decided. Like displaying the pocket watch—well, that had almost turned out disastrous—it was a big step, putting something that precious out in the open where she could look at it every day. Doing more than just committing it to memory.

But why the hell not? Whatever Lloyd's reason in giving it to her, she would ignore that and make it her own. If Emma O'Neill couldn't yet win the war, she would at least win a battle or two.

"Mondragon and O'Neill," Pete had said, still pondering their new business. "Alpha order."

"O'Neill and Mondragon," she countered. "Age order."

He'd laughed hard enough that she'd had to help him readjust his blue sling.

Now the sun was coming up. It was just before seven in the morning.

Emma zipped the lid on her suitcase, picked it up and carried it to the door. *One more sweep*, she thought. Make sure she didn't miss anything. And then her gaze caught the mess on the kitchen counter, strewn with Styrofoam coffee cups and doughnut crumbs.

She set down the suitcase and went to find a sponge. She was wiping the counter when she heard the knock.

"It's open," she said, then realized it probably wasn't. Pete had no key.

"You know you're a pain in the—"

The door swung open.

Charlie stood on the other side, very still, waiting, as was his way. His hair was a wild thatch on his head. His skin was tawny and smooth. He was tall and slender, his arms muscled, his jaw neatly defined. His eyes were a deeper brown than anyone else's.

"Emma," said Charlie Ryan.

The sponge dropped from her hand.

"Charlie," Emma said, and his name on her tongue sounded both foreign and familiar. She swallowed, feeling those two syllables rush through her. *Charlie. Charlie.* He was in her heart and veins and blood. He always had been, she realized. She had never lost him, not really.

He was *alive*. He was *here*. He wasn't dead.

"How?" She could barely form the question. He told her briefly. He'd tell her more later. There was time. *So much time.*

"I tried to find you," Emma said.

"Me, too," he said. "I was so stupid, Em, to leave you. I—"

"Shh," she whispered. She had forgiven him long ago. Now she forgave herself.

He looked at her.

"I became a private investigator," she said, as if that could explain a century of loss.

But he smiled. Not with his mouth, but with his eyes, with that sparkle nobody ever saw but her. "And I became—"

"A pilot," Emma finished with him.

They were flying then, both of them, the years and the sadness and the endless places rushing below them, as they soared above it all. Alligators and swamps and Fountains of Youth and Juan Ponce de León, dead by an arrow. Long-dead parents and siblings and a man named Glen Walters who tried and failed to destroy the threads that held them together. Murdered girls and one named Coral, alive if just barely, because Emma refused to give up. A happy boy named Hugo Alvarez. A huckster named Kingsley Lloyd who had given them a gift they never wanted and still barely understood. The people who had come and gone as Emma had traveled and hoped and wondered and lived. Sylvie Parsons in Chicago. A boy named Aaron Tinsley. Poor Elodie Callahan, whom Emma couldn't save. Pocket watches (beautiful and heavy) and hawks and constellations. Family. A baby brother Emma missed so much sometimes it was often hard to breathe. Even now. Even after so very, very long. A friend named Pete Mondragon, true as could be.

It rushed by them and through them, years and hours and minutes and seconds.

You never knew what was coming in this world, not really.

That was the true mystery, the true wonder. You just hung on and hoped for the best.

This boy. This boy.

Charlie stepped over the threshold, and he was smiling with his mouth now, and every false move, every empty hope, every reckless mistake—there had been so many—faded. Not gone, because these were the things that had led them here, the things that had changed them inexorably even as they remained the same.

Oh, thought Emma. *This is why. Because now. Because us.*

It wasn't what she expected. Not at all.

Her long-bruised heart swelled. *This boy. This man. This return.*

Charlie held out his arms, and she closed the distance between them.

Acknowledgments

It's a strange and wonderful task to write a story about immortality: A girl and a boy, in love and stuck at seventeen. A Fountain of Youth. The crazy, sad, happy, romantic, and dangerous hundred-year adventure that happens when they lose each other.

An American fairy tale, I told my editor.

And make it funny sometimes, he said.

No problem, I told him. *But I also want to make you cry. Because living forever, that would sometimes make you cry, right?*

Thank you times eternity to Daniel Ehrenhaft for believing I could write this book and giving me the time and copious editorial notes to get it right.

And to the entire Soho Press team, including but not limited to Bronwen Hruska, Juliet Grames, Rachel Kowal, Janine Agro, Meredith Barnes, Rudy Martinez and cover designer Christian Fuenfhausen—I am ever so lucky to be part of your astonishingly creative, nimble crew.

It is impossible to find enough thank yous for Jennifer Rofé, best agent ever, who encourages, supports, negotiates like a pit bull, and occasionally reminds me to get over my bad self.

To my lovely critique partners, especially Christina Mandelski, Varsha Bajaj, Colleen Thompson, and Kim O'Brien: thank you for endless encouragement with each draft—and there were a LOT of drafts.

Hugs to the author crew at Lodge of Death, the best writing retreat with insanely abundant taxidermy in Texas. I can't even . . . And thanks to my Houston writers, The YAHOUS, for enthusiastic cheerleading and generosity.

Another round of thanks to every blogger and bookseller and librarian who has supported me and my books. I absolutely could not do this without you.

And as always to Rick, Jake, and Kellie: I love you all forever and forever.